D1409202

Eenie, Meanie, Murphy, NO!

March 1, 1991

Best Wishes Jennifer for lots of happy reading! Fondly, Colleen O'Shaughnessy McKenna

Other books by
Colleen O'Shaughnessy McKenna

Too Many Murphys

Fourth Grade Is a Jinx

Fifth Grade: Here Comes Trouble

Eenie, Meanie, Murphy, NO!

Colleen O'Shaughnessy McKenna

Scholastic Inc.
New York

Copyright © 1990 by Colleen O'Shaughnessy McKenna.
All rights reserved. Published by Scholastic Inc.
SCHOLASTIC HARDCOVER is a registered trademark of Scholastic Inc.

No part of this publication may be reproduced in whole or in part, or stored in a retrieval system, or transmitted in any form or by any means, electronic, mechanical, photocopying, recording, or otherwise, without written permission of the publisher. For information regarding permission, write to Scholastic Inc., 730 Broadway, New York, NY 10003.

Library of Congress Cataloging-in-Publication Data
McKenna, Colleen O'Shaughnessy.
Eenie, meanie, Murphy, no / Colleen O'Shaughnessy McKenna.
p. cm.
Summary: While at camp Collette is desperate to retrieve her secret diary, which has been stolen and read out loud.

ISBN 0-590-42899-3

[1. Diaries—Fiction. 2. Camps—Fiction.] I. Title.
PZ7.M478675Ee 1990
[Fic]—dc20 89-10626
CIP
AC

12 11 10 9 8 7 6 5 4 3 2 1 0 1 2 3 4 5/9

Printed in the U.S.A. 37

First Scholastic printing, April 1990

Lovingly dedicated to
Joe, Sherrie, Michelle,
and their wonderful families.
Thanks for the memories.

Chapter One

"Mom, we are two hours late for camp already!" said Collette, trying to keep her voice calm. "Maybe we missed our exit. I don't think you were watching the signs when Stevie threw his bologna sandwich out the window."

"I didn't miss the exit," said her mother. She looked in the rearview mirror and smiled at Collette. "Don't worry."

"I *had* to throw that sandwich away," Stevie insisted. "Jeff said a fly spitted on it."

"Here are some more signs now," their mother said cheerfully. "Okay, guys, get ready to read them off to me."

Collette groaned and crossed her arms. She was

never going to get to Calvary Camp at this rate. It was already two o'clock, and camp still seemed a million miles away.

"I'm carsick!" wailed Laura. She stuck her head out the window. "Are we almost there?"

"Get in here, Laura," cried Collette. "Do you want to fall out in the middle of the turnpike?"

"Yeah, and don't throw up out the window or we'll look like a bunch of jerks," added Jeff.

"Laura, sit down and buckle up," said their mother. "I'll get you a root beer in a minute or two. Jeff, quick, read me these signs as we go past."

"Restrooms, tourist information, food. *Food!* Oh, great! Mom, let's stop; I'm starving."

"I'm carsick," cried Laura. "My stomach is bubbling."

"Well, I'm *really* sick," added Stevie. "I think I ate some fly spit."

Collette laughed at Stevie. He was five years old and copied everyone, no matter what.

"You're okay, Stevie. Jeff is only teasing." Collette reached over and hugged him.

"No sir, Stevie," continued Jeff with a huge grin

on his face. "If you ate fly spit, that means you'll turn into a fly in less than an hour, right, Mom?"

Collette saw her mother try not to smile.

"Don't tease, Jeff."

Stevie unbuckled his seat belt and flew forward. "Mommy, am I turning into a fly?"

"You'll have to live in a garbage can," snickered Jeff. "Or else Dad will get the fly swatter after you."

"Mommy!" wailed Stevie. "I don't want to live in a garbage can!"

Collette smiled and leaned back against her seat. Her brothers were always wrestling and teasing each other. Jeff thought it was a nine-year-old's duty to tease any five-year-old in the room.

Today it didn't bother Collette too much. She was on her way to camp.

Camp! Collette leaned forward, nervous all over again. Why was it taking so long to *get* to camp? Everyone else would already be there, sitting in their cabins and wondering if Collette Murphy would ever show up.

"Maybe we should get off at the next exit," suggested Mrs. Murphy. "I had two cups of coffee before we left, and I am ready to float right out of this car."

Collette tapped her mother on the shoulder. "Do we *have* to stop, Mom? We are *already* so late for camp. There might be some sort of deadline for checking in."

Her mother just laughed as she put on the blinker.

"They don't have deadlines for camp, Collette. Just relax, sweetie. We'll get there."

Collette sighed as she slid back into her seat. Sure they'd get there, but when?

She smiled at her mother in the rearview mirror. It wasn't her mother's fault the trip was taking so long.

"I'm starving," Jeff grumbled. "We got up so early, and the sandwich you packed was stale."

"I'm starving, too," added Stevie.

"You *said* you were carsick, Stevie," Collette reminded him. "Don't eat if you're sick."

"More of me is hungry than sick."

Collette stared out the window and shook her head. She just knew she was going to be the *very last person* to drive into camp. Then the whole camp would know she was part of a *big, disorganized family* that never made it anywhere on time.

Once she got to camp Collette knew things would be perfect. But so far everything that could have gone wrong had gone wrong. First, her dad had called from Wisconsin. His law meetings were running late, so he couldn't be home in time to drive Collette to camp. That meant her mother had had to climb all the way up to the attic to drag down granddad's old army trunk. Then she'd had to borrow a neighbor's luggage rack and wrestle it to the top of the car.

It fell off.

Twice.

Finally Mrs. Murphy had had to borrow the neighbor to fasten the rack onto the car.

Packing all the kids into the car had caused even more trouble. Nobody but Mother had wanted to drive three and a half hours in a hot car to deposit Collette at camp.

Collette twisted her ring around and around her finger, trying not to feel ungrateful. Her mom was trying so hard to keep everyone in a good mood.

She obviously wanted Collette to have a great send-off for camp.

It would have been so much easier if Collette had just taken the bus up with her best friend, Sarah. Lots of other kids from Sacred Heart took the chartered bus.

Collette had even suggested it. But her mother hadn't liked the idea at all. She'd said, "You're only eleven years old, Collette, which is much too young to deliver yourself to camp. Besides, this is your first time away from home, and I want to see where you'll be staying."

Collette smiled now. She knew how much her mom was going to miss her. She would miss her, too, and her dad, and even her brothers and little sister, Laura.

But the long, noisy car ride was making her even more anxious to begin a relaxing week at camp.

"Are you going to be real homesick?" asked Laura. She squirmed a little closer and leaned her head against Collette.

Collette looked down at Laura's pale face and tried not to laugh. She looked around the crowded car, filled with hungry and carsick kids.

No, she probably wouldn't be homesick or scared. Not for a minute.

She was on her way to Calvary Camp. Surrounded by tall pine trees, with shady horseback riding trails and a huge blue lake . . . and not one little Murphy to get in the way. No little brothers wrestling in front of her friends; no little sister begging to tag along.

Camp was going to be heaven!

Best of all, she would be spending the week with her best friend, Sarah. Marsha Cessano would be there, too, but even she couldn't put a damper on things.

Marsha lived right across the street from Collette and was sometimes more a neighbor than a friend. She often made Collette mad, bragging about how lucky she was to have been born an only child. And a rich one at that.

"Mommy, I am really ready to throw up now," whimpered Laura in a shaky voice. "Jeff keeps eating those stinky Mexican corn chips. Now the whole car smells."

"Give me some of them corn chips," cried

Stevie, springing out of his seat belt and dangling over the seat.

"Ask nicely, Stevie," reminded their mother. "Oh, good, here's a gas station."

"Are you going to ask them where camp is?" asked Collette hopefully. She swatted Stevie's tennis shoes out of her face and tried to look out the window. "Is this our exit?"

Please let it be my exit, she prayed.

"Our exit is still up the road, Collette. I thought we could stop for a few Cokes and rest up a bit."

Rest up a bit? How much more rested could they get? They had been sitting in the car for hours and hours.

"Mom, we are going to be so late it isn't even funny!" Collette announced. She leaned forward to plead her case. "The camp letter said that we should get there by noon. What if they just gave my spot to someone else? Someone who followed their rules?"

Mrs. Murphy grinned. Collette sank back in her seat. Her mother was laughing about everything. Arriving late at camp wasn't funny! Collette could just picture the camp director frowning down at his clipboard and shaking his head at the late Murphys.

"No more room, kid. Try being on time next year if you want to go to camp!"

Mrs. Murphy stopped the car in the shade of a thick grove of trees at the edge of the parking lot. Everyone except for Collette scrambled to get out of the car.

"Jeff, there are plenty of quarters in my change purse. Why don't you start getting some cold drinks out of the machine, and I'll sit with Laura over by the picnic tables?"

"Me, too," cried Stevie. "I'm the sickest."

"You are not," muttered Laura. "I keep burping, which is almost like throwing up, right, Mommy?"

"Oh, yeah?" Stevie raced over and frowned up in Laura's face. "Well I ate fly spit, and that's real bad."

Collette leaned over and slammed the car door. She wasn't even going to get out of the car. Reaching down, she took her new diary out of her backpack. She pulled out the tiny, thin pencil and scribbled her first entry.

Sunday afternoon

Dear Diary,

I am already two hours late for camp because of my slow family.

"Stevie!" shouted his mother. "Stevie Murphy!"

Collette dropped her diary and poked her head out the window. Stevie was standing in freshly tarred pavement.

"Get out of that tar this minute, young man!" Mrs. Murphy ordered.

Stevie took two sticky steps before he stopped.

"I'm glued down!" he yelled at the top of his lungs. "I'm stuck all the way!"

Mrs. Murphy raced over and pulled Stevie by the shirt sleeve to the side of the tar. "Just *look* at your new tennis shoes! You can't even get back in the car with that tar all over you."

Stevie looked alarmed. He glanced from the car to his mother before bursting into tears.

"But I *want* to get in the car," he wailed loudly. "I don't want to live at the gas station."

Jeff started to laugh as he took another can from the machine. He pointed at Stevie. "Hah, little gas station man!"

Collette leaned her head in her hands. Great! Another Murphy crisis! It would take at least five minutes for Mrs. Murphy to convince Stevie that he didn't have to live at the gas station, then another twenty more to scrape the tar from his shoes. After that, it would take a good *hour* to load everyone back into the car so they could get going.

What else could happen to add another hour to the trip? A flash flood? A hurricane spinning down the turnpike. . . ?

"Mommy!" Laura screamed. "Help! Oh, yuck!"

Collette opened the car door and looked toward the picnic tables. Laura yelped again before she bent down and threw up an entire can of root beer.

"Oh, Laura!" cried Collette. She grabbed the

box of tissues from the front seat and raced across the parking lot. Poor Laura was doubled over again, hanging on to a huge trash can with one shaking hand.

"You'll feel better in a minute, Laura," Collette said gently as she patted her on the back. "I'll buy you some gum in the gas station."

Collette glanced behind at the cars streaming past. Everyone was going someplace but the Murphys.

It was going to take forever to get to Calvary Camp. Maybe even longer.

Chapter Two

Sunday afternoon

Dear Diary,

We are almost at camp. Laura is asleep on my lap, and the boys are being good for a change. I will miss them a lot. (Ha-Ha).

Well, I guess I will miss them a little. They all wrote me notes and put them in my trunk.

Well, my—

☺

"Here we are, children!" called Mrs. Murphy from the front seat. "Calvary Camp at last!"

The car wheels crunched slowly down the dusty gravel road. Cabins were set deep in the trees on either side.

Collette leaned forward, lowering Laura's head gently onto the seat. Laura had been asleep ever since the car had pulled away from the gas station.

"Hey, this place is really cool," declared Jeff. "Maybe I can come to camp next year."

Collette only nodded, closing her diary and locking it. She didn't want to encourage Jeff too much. Camp was going to be *her* private territory for as long as possible. The fewer Murphys, the better.

Collette loved her brothers and little sister, she really did. But being the oldest of four was a lot of work . . . helping Jeff with his homework, trying to convince Laura not to suck her thumb, or stopping Stevie from riding his bike in the living room.

Camp was going to be her *private* vacation.

"Just look at that blue lake," her mother pointed out. "Oh, I wish we could all stay!"

"Can we?" asked Stevie. "My shoes are real clean now."

Collette was relieved when her mother laughed. "No, not this year, Stevie. You're only five years old."

"Will that lake still be here when I'm bigger?" He looked worried as he stared out the window.

"Sure it will," Collette promised. "And Stevie, guess what? I'm going to make you something special in my craft class. Do you want an Indian headband, with real blue and white beads?"

Stevie grinned and nodded. "And make me a bow and arrow, too."

"Craft class," said her mother dreamily. "I can still remember making pot holders for my mother. Green and red for Christmas . . . oh, Collette, you are going to have so much fun! Be sure and write everything down in your diary. You did pack your new diary, didn't you?"

"It's right here." Collette rubbed her hand over the smooth, glossy blue diary. It was brand new, with a bright gold lock and matching key. On its cover a small white kitten peered above a red ball of yarn, a tiny crayon propped in its paw.

As soon as she got into her cabin she would have to find a safe place for the key. This diary was going to be private. She didn't want Marsha trying to read it all the time.

Collette moved closer to the window, making sure she didn't bother Laura. She didn't want to jolt her and have her start crying. It would be so embarrassing to pull up in front of her cabin with a car full of noisy Murphys. She wanted to make a good impression.

"What's your cabin number?" asked Jeff.

"I don't know. Marsha came up with her parents last night so she would be the first one here and could pick out the best cabin."

Mrs. Murphy laughed. "Mrs. Cessano made reservations at a huge fancy hotel nearby. She wanted Marsha to have one last night of sleeping on ironed sheets before she had to endure a week of bunk beds."

"Marsha's spoiled rotten," Jeff mumbled from the front seat. "No wonder she's a jerk."

"Jeff," their mother warned.

"She is," insisted Jeff. "You should have heard her making fun of Granddad's old army trunk. She said Collette was going to look like a bag lady walking into camp with it."

Collette frowned as she remembered. Marsha had barged into their house the night before she left, camp supply list in hand. She had marched around like a general, making sure Collette had remembered everything.

"I've been to camp once before, Collette, so I am kind of an expert," she'd announced while walking around and around Granddad's faded green trunk, a slight sneer on her face.

"Is *this* the trunk you're taking, Collette?"

"Of course it is, Marsha. You can see all my clothes packed in it."

Marsha had just raised her eyebrows as if she were totally surprised.

"What's wrong with my trunk?"

Marsha gave the trunk a slight kick, as if to check the air in a tire, and shrugged.

"Nothing's *wrong* with it . . . I guess."

Collette sighed, hoping Marsha would be in a good mood at camp.

"Here's the office. We can check for your cabin number," said Mrs. Murphy. She turned off the engine and opened the door.

Collette slid out from under Laura and stood in

the sun. As she shielded her eyes, she watched other campers walking in groups of twos and threes.

Everyone looked so happy. They were walking as if they knew exactly where they were going and what they were going to do. Calvary Camp looked so nice and grown up.

Collette drew her diary closer to her chest. She didn't know where she was going at all. This was her first time at camp. . . . Luckily it was Sarah's first time at Calvary, too. What if they couldn't catch on to things fast enough? What if the other kids made fun of them? Would they send them down with the younger kids? Marsha had said the littlest kids were called rug rats.

Collette shuddered, knowing she would hate to be part of the rodent group.

"Jeff, Stevie, stay near the car in case Laura wakes up," called Mrs. Murphy. She raced up the three wooden steps to the office. "Come on, Collette. Let's find out where your cabin is."

Collette followed her mother into the office, making sure she didn't miss a thing. A large bulletin board filled with notices covered one wall.

In the center, a huge yellow sign was posted:

CAMP'S LAST HURRAH!
FRIDAY BANQUET
DINNER 7:00 DANCING TILL 11:00

" 'Dancing till eleven,' " read Collette, glad she had packed her best sundress. She had never been to a real dance before. At Sacred Heart Elementary, you had to wait until seventh grade before you were allowed to go to a dance.

Beside the large wooden desk, Mrs. Murphy was already talking to a large balding man in baggy khaki shorts. He had a silver whistle dangling from his neck, a worn-looking baseball cap on his head.

"Murphy . . . Murphy," he chanted as he ran a tanned finger down a sheet of paper. "Cabin seven . . . the other girls checked in hours ago."

Collette pulled her head back to stare at the bulletin board, embarrassed. . . . Of course, Marsha and Sarah checked in hours ago. Collette was *hours late.*

"Cabin seven is past the mess hall and a quick

right up the hill. Follow the yellow trail signs. Number's posted on the outside."

Mrs. Murphy put her arm around Collette as they walked back out into the bright sunlight.

"Now what am I going to do without you for a whole week, Collette?"

Collette smiled.

"It's not too late to hop back in the car with your old mom and head back to Pittsburgh."

"Mom," giggled Collette.

"Need any help getting the trunk down, ladies?"

Collette looked up, staring right into the eyes of a tall, muscular boy. He looked at least thirteen or maybe even fourteen. While he wasn't wearing a counselor's shirt or whistle, he acted as if he were in charge.

"Thanks," said her mother. "I didn't know how I was going to get it down. Be careful, it's very heavy."

"No problem," he laughed, swinging the trunk down easily.

Collette reached into her shorts, got out her new

sunglasses, and pushed them on. Her hand almost shook with nervousness.

With his short blond hair and huge arms, this boy was so handsome, it was almost like talking to a movie star. Had the camp rented him to walk around just looking perfect?

"Do you work here during the summers?" asked Mrs. Murphy.

Collette tilted her head, waiting for the answer, hoping it was yes. Usually it embarrassed her when her mother talked too much to strangers, especially boy strangers.

But today she was glad. Today she wanted the answers, too.

"No, I'm only thirteen," the boy laughed. "I live in town, so I've been coming to camp for years. It's like my second home."

He smiled down at Collette. "Is this your first year?"

Collette nodded, glad her sunglasses hid the fear in her eyes. Did it show that much? Was she wearing first-time-camper clothes or something?

"I'd better wake up Laura," her mother said as

she opened the car door. "Come on, Laura. Time to wake up and go see Collette's cabin."

"Boy, are you a strong man!" cried Stevie. "Like Popeye!"

"Be quiet, Stevie," grumbled Jeff. "Boy, do you say dumb things."

But the boy just laughed, reaching out and grabbing Stevie around the waist. "Yeah, I lift little guys like you fifty times a day." He held Stevie up above his head for a couple of seconds.

As soon as he put Stevie down, he picked up the trunk and started walking.

"Where to?"

"Cabin seven," croaked Collette. She cleared the frog in her throat and hoped Jeff wouldn't make a crack.

"Can I touch your muscle?" asked Stevie, his pointing finger already in midair.

"You are such a jerk, Stevie," exploded Jeff. He pulled his baseball cap down over his eyes, falling a step or two behind, so nobody would know he was with them.

"Hey, it's okay," laughed the boy again. "My little cousins do this to me all the time. I lift weights, so I'm used to questions from kids."

"See?" cried Stevie to Jeff. "He wants me to!" He reached out and touched the boy's arm. "It feels like your arm swallowed a rock!"

"I hope that trunk isn't too heavy," said Mrs. Murphy. "Collette packed enough for a month."

Collette cringed, praying her mother wouldn't list everything inside the trunk . . . ten shorts, three shortie pajamas, twenty cotton panties, all with her name inked in.

As they neared the steps of the cabin, she looked over at the trunk, then quickly away.

Marsha had been right!

In the sunlight the trunk did seem drab, battered. It looked like it had been through World War I. Somebody as handsome as this boy should only carry brand-new trunks.

"What's your name?" asked Stevie. He was walking in step with the boy now, stretching out his legs to keep up. "My name is Stevie, but when I turn six I am going to tell people to call me Steve."

"Stevie . . . nice name."

They all walked in silence for another few yards.

Behind her, Collette could hear her mother talking softly to Laura, pointing out birds and wildflowers.

Nobody but Collette was aware that the boy had forgotten to tell Stevie his name.

Ask him again, she wanted to shout.

"What's *your* name?"

Collette nearly jumped. Was he talking to her? She grinned, relieved, when she realized the boy was asking Jeff.

"Jeff . . . Jeff Murphy . . . I'm almost ten."

Collette opened her mouth to remind Jeff that he had just turned nine less than a month ago. But she didn't want the boy to think she was a know-it-all older sister.

"Cabin seven!" announced the boy. He carried the trunk up the stairs and waited for Collette to open the door.

"You'd better go in first and check. I don't want to . . . surprise anybody."

He grinned down at her. Collette thought her heart was going to fly right out of her mouth. Up close she could see the yellow flecks in his green eyes. And as she reached across to push open the screen, she could smell his peppermint gum and suntan lotion.

As soon as she entered the dark cool cabin, she was charged by Marsha and Sarah.

"Where have you *been*? Someone tried to kill us!" cried Marsha.

Mrs. Murphy pushed the door open and the boy walked in, setting down the trunk with a heavy *thump*.

As soon as he straightened up, stretching both arms back to relax his muscles, Marsha yelped. She was staring at him with her mouth open as if a statue had suddenly come to life right in front of her.

"Thank you so much," said Mrs. Murphy. She smiled at the boy and extended her hand. "I'm Mrs. Murphy and this is Laura. You've already met Jeff and Stevie, and this is our camper, Collette."

Collette cringed. Camper Collette. It made her sound like she should be marching up and down Sesame Street with Big Bird and Ernie.

"I'm Marsha Cessano." Marsha moved right up and stood next to the trunk. "I went to an expensive camp in Massachusetts last year. That's why you don't know me already."

"And this is Sarah Messland," added Collette. She reached out and shoved Sarah in between the boy and Marsha.

The boy nodded and smiled. "Hi. Name's Tommy Hansley."

Marsha nodded, mouthing his name as though she were committing it to memory for life.

Stevie climbed on top of the trunk and tapped Tommy on the chest. "Won't your mommy let kids call you Tom yet?"

Everyone laughed. Marsha reached over and messed up Stevie's curly blond hair.

"Children . . . don't you just love what they say?"

Stevie ducked out from under Marsha's hand and stood closer to Tommy.

Mrs. Murphy sat on a bunk bed and pulled Marsha down next to her. "Marsha, sit down and tell me more about the person who tried to . . . to murder you?"

"Yeah," said Jeff, getting interested. "Some sort of camp mugger?"

Marsha's eyes grew large. "Exactly! Three

muggers came after me. One was so large she could have snapped my neck off."

Collette smiled. Marsha was always exaggerating everything. A fat girl had probably just bumped into Marsha accidentally.

"The tall girl was named Peal or Penny or Peally. Anyway, she said that I couldn't have this cabin, even though I had my trunk in here first. I was the first camper here."

Tommy began to laugh.

"That must be Peally Jackson. Long blonde hair?"

Marsha nodded. "Peally said that she has had cabin seven since she was eight years old and that it was *her* official cabin. She said I should get out or she'd use me as an anchor for her sailboat!"

Jeff and Stevie started to laugh.

"Is she dangerous?" asked Mrs. Murphy. Collette could tell her mother was a little worried. Maybe so worried she would ask Tommy to drag the trunk back down to the car so Collette could return to Pittsburgh.

"Peally is okay," Tommy said quickly. "She just has a big mouth and a bad temper."

Marsha's eyebrows shot up. Collette smiled. Kids at Sacred Heart had said the same thing about Marsha ever since kindergarten. But Marsha's temper wasn't dangerous. And she would never deliberately try to hurt anyone.

"Well, I don't like the idea of her threatening the girls," continued Mrs. Murphy. "Maybe I should talk to the counselor."

"Mom!" Collette wailed. She instantly heard that her voice came out too high, too loud, but she didn't care. She would *die* if her mother ran to the counselor and tattled on another girl.

The whole camp would whisper about Collette Murphy, everyone wishing she had never come to Calvary Camp in the first place.

She might even end up as an anchor on the bottom of the lake.

"Don't worry, Mrs. Murphy," assured Tommy. "Peally and I go back a long way. I'll talk to her. Besides, I'll be glad to keep an eye on the girls for you."

"Especially me!" blurted out Marsha. "I'm the one they threatened!"

"And watch out for Collette, Tommy," added

Laura. She tugged on Tommy's hand until he looked down. "She's the only sister I've got."

Tommy tapped Laura on the end of her nose and nodded.

"Okay. Don't worry. She'll be in one piece when you come to pick her up."

Opening the screen door, Tommy flashed another lopsided grin.

"See you," he said slowly as he left.

"See you!" the three girls chanted back in unison. Silence hung in the room as they all listened to Tommy run down the path.

Collette slid down on the faded green trunk and smiled. It had taken a long time to get to camp, but it had been worth every mile. Camp was great!

Chapter Three

Sunday afternoon

Dear Diary,

There's trouble at camp already!! Marsha said a girl named Peally is mad at us because we took her favorite cabin!!! I'll tell you more later...

The good news is that the most handsome boy in the world has promised to watch over me at camp. His name is Tommy Hansley, and he...

"You're not even listening to me!" accused Marsha. She whacked her fist down on a bunk bed's mattress.

"Yes, I am." Collette closed her diary and locked it. Marsha had been talking nonstop ever since Mrs. Murphy had left camp. Collette had just tried to sneak a few lines in her diary before she forgot.

"Listen to me, Collette. We're in big trouble," Marsha continued. She was beginning to pace up and down the length of the cabin, stopping now and then to peer out a window.

"Those girls mean business!" added Sarah. She shivered. "I was so scared."

"But why did they think they could just come right into our cabin?" asked Collette. She looked around the small cabin. It looked safe enough to her. And it certainly wasn't so fancy that another camper would try to come in and reclaim it.

"Peally wants this cabin, and she's willing to kill to get it," snapped Marsha.

Collette giggled. Marsha loved being dramatic about everything.

Sarah flopped down on the bed next to Collette

and rolled her eyes. "Well, that may be exaggerating it a little, Marsha — "

Marsha flew across the room like a dart. "Exaggerating? How can I exaggerate the fact that Peally told me to let her have this cabin or she would remove my face?"

Collette and Sarah started to giggle, then laugh, and finally shriek as they watched Marsha get madder and madder.

Marsha blew her bangs straight up in the air, then yanked them down again. "I don't believe you two. I was the one who made my parents get up at six o'clock this morning so I could get the best cabin for us. I was the first one in line, and now I have my very face threatened, and you two just laugh. I wouldn't laugh if I were you, Collette."

Collette sat up straighter and tried to look appreciative.

"I know, and it was nice of you to come up early. But really, Marsha . . ." Collette waved her hand around the small cabin. "If Peally wants the cabin so badly, let her have it."

Collette hated to fight about things.

Marsha shook her head and crossed her arms tightly in front of her chest. "No way. I staked my claim. Cabin seven is ours! This cabin is the best."

Sarah pointed to the door. "Actually, we do have a *red* door. All the other cabins have blue. And this cabin only has two sets of bunk beds, and the other cabins have three or four."

"It's as close to a condo as we're going to get up here," added Marsha seriously. "I want privacy. I don't want to share a cabin with two complete strangers who would just love to hear the private details of my life."

Collette nodded. She wanted privacy, too, especially since she never had it at home with her two brothers and little sister.

"I just don't want to be stuck with a nerd or gossip, who would blab our secrets all over camp," confided Marsha.

Collette giggled. She wasn't sure she had any secrets to blab.

"Oh sure, go ahead and start laughing again, Collette Murphy," Marsha shouted. She took a step closer to Collette, one hand on her hip and the other extended like a pistol. "I did my very best to get us this special, isolated cabin and all you did was arrive very, *very* late with a tribe of little Murphys!"

Collette stiffened. Marsha never missed a chance to remind her that she had two too many brothers and a little sister who trailed Collette like a shadow.

"Okay, let's not fight." Sarah said gently. Sarah was always nice to everyone. She was proof that not all only children were spoiled like Marsha.

"The way I see it, we've got to work out a plan, or our whole week here will be miserable. . . ." began Marsha.

"Yeah," laughed Sarah. "I don't want to hide in our cabin all week."

"Peally caught us off guard, which is why we panicked," said Marsha. She peered out the window again, as if expecting tanks outside.

"Coast is clear. Now listen, girls. The first thing we do is play our high card."

"What?" cried Collette and Sarah. They

watched Marsha strut back and forth like a drill sergeant.

"We'll show them that we are not to be messed with. Maybe we can . . . well, beat them at tennis or . . ."

Collette laughed. "Marsha, that wouldn't scare them. I have a better idea. Why don't we just try being nice to them and then — "

Marsha's loud groan made Collette start.

"Camp is no place for marshmallows, Collette. We fight fire with fire."

"Marsha, a tennis match is not fire." Sarah reminded her.

The cabin was silent as the three digested that. Collette glanced over at Sarah, hoping to see a smile. But Sarah was busy chewing her cuticle and looking worried.

Outside a loud bell rang.

"Dinner," explained Marsha. "This will be the first encounter. Get ready for any sort of surprise attack."

"Marsha," Sarah groaned. "Stop talking like that. I am getting really nervous about all this.

Peally's friend was huge. Her wrist was the size of my thigh."

"So don't arm wrestle her," laughed Collette.

Marsha and Sarah both looked at Collette. There wasn't a smile in sight.

"Collette, wait until you see how mean those girls can get," warned Sarah. "Sacred Heart doesn't even *have* kids this mean."

Marsha stood up and rubbed her hands together.

"Let's go, girls. Remember, follow my lead."

Collette and Sarah grinned at each other. Marsha was acting like a protective mother bear. By the time they reached the dining hall, all three girls were laughing again.

"I bet that girl Peally and her friends have forgotten all about you by now." Collette held open the heavy wooden door. "Smells good in here. Maybe camp food isn't so bad."

"I think we get our trays over there," Sarah said, pointing to a long line near the wall.

"Oh, no . . . look who's at the head of the line! *Peally!*" Marsha dug her nails into Collette's arm.

"Where?"

"That blonde in the blue and white sweatshirt," Sarah pointed out.

Across the row of tables, Collette watched as Peally and her two friends walked through the serving line and sat down.

"They look normal," Collette whispered. She had been expecting a trio of mud wrestlers.

"Hah!" snorted Marsha as she grabbed a tray. "Wait till they find out which cabin you're in, Collette. Then their eyes turn wild and smoke comes out their noses."

As Collette collected her dinner, she watched the three girls. They were just laughing and eating. Normal stuff. She walked past their table, almost smiling as she thought of how Marsha had exaggerated the whole situation.

"Oh, look. This must be the missing third camper," said the largest girl. She pushed her chair out and stood up in Collette's path.

Collette couldn't help but stare at the girl's thick wrist. She was gripping a fork so tightly her knuckles were white against her skin.

"Now the three stooges are complete," added the girl called Peally. She stood up next to her friend. "Aren't they cute, Linda?" she cooed.

Marsha gave the girls her best glare and continued moving. Sarah let out a soft whimper before hurrying after her.

Collette knew it was always better to start out with good manners. She took a deep breath, looked up, and smiled.

"Hi. I'm Collette Murphy . . ."

"Well, lah-di-dah!" hooted the third girl. She was thin with long, stringy, brown hair. "Now I can die happy. I met Collette Murphy!"

Collette looked ahead, hoping Marsha and Sarah were close.

These rude girls gave her the creeps already. Maybe they should give them back their crummy cabin. Then they would be happy and leave them alone. She took a few steps forward.

"Look, the little rug rat is running away," called Peally. She laughed loudly, which seemed to trigger the others to start laughing.

Complete strangers looked up from their pork and beans and started to snicker. Glad to laugh, glad it wasn't them being laughed at.

"Hey, Murphy!" called a familiar voice.

Collette almost dropped her tray in surprise. Turning to the left she saw Roger Friday zooming across the room with his tray.

"Roger, what are you doing here?"

He wore a huge T-shirt with AND I'M RICH, TOO printed in large blue letters. It hung almost to the end of his orange-and-green plaid shorts. His blue baseball cap had the rim shoved straight up and a yellow propeller on top.

Collette grinned. Roger had never looked better to her in his life.

"What's wrong?" Roger asked. He wasn't smiling or ready to make a funny crack like he always did in school. "Are you okay, Collette?"

"Oh, those girls . . ." began Collette. She stopped quickly, hearing how near to tears she was.

Roger peered behind her, scowling at the girls, who were busy whispering behind their hands.

"Ah, ignore them. They probably just drank too much lake water."

Collette nodded her head up and down rapidly. She didn't even think anyone else from school would be at Calvary Camp. It was Presbyterian, and most of the kids from Sacred Heart ended up at Holy Rosary Camp in Ligoneer.

"I see you brought Marsha," said Roger in a hoarse voice. "My favorite person." He wiggled his eyebrows up and down until Collette finally had to smile.

Roger and Marsha had been having a great time fighting and getting each other into trouble since kindergarten.

"I'm in cabin twenty-one if you need a body-guard," offered Roger. He laughed as if it were a joke, his ears turning pink. But Collette knew he was using his serious voice. "In fact, I have a whole table full of friends, Collette," he added. "If you need anything . . ."

"I'm okay. Well — I'd better go sit down," said Collette. She was about to say, "Thank you," to Roger for trying to make her feel better. But she didn't.

He might think she was nuts.

"Oh lookee here, Linda. Little Miss Rug Rat has herself a boyfriend," cooed Peally as she carried her tray past. "Isn't that adorable? I bet they'll carve their initials in a tree!"

"Rug rat's blushing," added the thin girl in a nasty whine. "I didn't know a rat could blush."

Collette blinked quickly, feeling her cheeks getting warmer and warmer.

"And I didn't think it was possible for a little rat to like a boy," added Linda. She bumped her large elbow into Collette's back as she thundered by. "I thought they just liked cheese. . . ."

"And stealing other people's *cabins*," added Peally. "We didn't know rug rats were thieves!"

Roger stared after them for just a second before he cupped his hands and called out, "You girls didn't *know* all that because you're just plain stupid!"

The dining hall was church quiet for a minute. Then the whole place broke up into loud laughing and claps.

Peally froze at Roger's words. When she finally turned to face Collette, her eyes still held the ice.

"You like hearing them laugh? Listen to it real good, creep. 'Cause the next time you hear it, they're gonna be laughing at you and your stupid friends."

"Get lost, motor mouth!" Roger ordered. He

ducked his head and twirled his propeller as the room exploded with more laughter.

Peally narrowed her eyes and looked at Collette, then over to where Marsha and Sarah sat.

"I'll be seeing you all real soon — that's a promise!"

As Peally stormed out of the dining hall, Collette tried to swallow.

Roger turned to Collette, red-faced, smiling, as proud as if he had just thrown his cloak over a large mud puddle for her.

Collette was too stricken to tell him he had just signed her death warrant at Calvary Camp.

Chapter Four

"Collette, I don't believe what I just saw!" cried Marsha. "We are in even more trouble than before!" She whacked her bun down so hard the hot dog bounced once before it rolled across the table and onto the floor.

"What did I do?" Collette asked. She slid into the seat next to Sarah. Her knees were still shaking.

Marsha looked up. She leaned across the table until she was nose to nose with Collette.

"You stopped to talk to Roger. That was your *first* big mistake. That lunatic boy got Peally and her gang madder than ever."

Sarah patted Collette on the shoulder. "It wasn't her fault. Roger came up to her, Marsha."

Collette nodded. She stared down at her food, knowing she couldn't force down a bite. Her stomach was tied up in so many knots it felt like a garden hose.

"Eat," barked out Marsha, her mouth full of french fries. "We'll need our strength now more than ever."

Sarah picked up her hot dog but closed her mouth and set it back down again. She gave Collette a weak smile.

"Maybe we should go pack and call our moms."

Collette sat up straighter and took a french fry. "Hey, don't say that, Sarah. We've been waiting for camp to start for months. Don't worry about Peally and her friends. I don't think they are going to bother us anymore." Collette smiled again, glad to see Marsha and Sarah both grinning back.

Marsha bit into an apple and chewed furiously. She looked out across the cafeteria, not seeming a bit scared. Things would be fine with Marsha. Marsha seemed to thrive, almost blossom, at the first sign of conflict.

"Sarah, camps have rules," Collette continued. "Their insurance policies tell them that kids can't fight or touch each other or . . ."

"Or use someone as an anchor," filled in Sarah, beginning to laugh.

The other girls joined in.

"My dad knows all that stuff since he's a lawyer. Camps have extra counselors just walking around to make sure nobody is planning to break a few rules. If one family sued a camp, it would be out of business."

Collette stopped, wondering what else she could add to make Sarah feel better. This was supposed to be a special week, and Collette was going to enjoy it, no matter what. Once the activities got started, Peally would forget all about the feud.

Collette looked up, watching Marsha as she quickly dropped her apple, wiped her mouth, and tried to smooth down her hair. All in less than two seconds.

"Marsha," giggled Collette. "What are you doing?"

"Hi."

As soon as she looked up, Collette knew why

Marsha was trying to fix herself up.

Tommy Hansley stood beside their table. He had changed into a pale blue sweatshirt, which made his blond hair seem even lighter.

"Tommy," said Marsha softly. She smiled sweetly. "Hello."

"Hey, you girls aren't eating," Tommy pointed out. He was looking right at Collette.

Marsha looked down at her ravished tray, apple cores and half-eaten french fries strewn all over. Collette tried not to smirk as Marsha quickly spread her napkin over the remains.

"Don't worry, breakfast will be better. It's boxed cereal," Tommy assured her. "They can't ruin that."

Collette nodded, thinking how very nice and polite Tommy was.

"Did you see Peally and her gang trying to upset Collette?" asked Marsha. She pushed up her sleeves and put both elbows on the table. "I hope you're still interested in protecting us, Tommy. I think we're going to need it."

"Sure. Count on me as your personal bodyguard."

The girls watched as he gave them a slight bow and walked slowly out of the dining hall.

Collette's fingers almost twitched. She wanted to run back and get her diary before she forgot a single word — "personal bodyguard . . ."

"I'm going to come back here every year," sighed Sarah. "I wonder if Tommy goes with anyone at camp."

"Peally."

All three girls jumped. The voice belonged to a short, dark girl about their age. She sat down next to them without even waiting to be asked. She ran her fingers through her black curly hair and smiled.

"Hi. I'm Amber. Peally has been in love with Tommy for two years. I thought you might want to know. So . . . hands off."

Collette frowned. How could that be? Tommy was so nice. Why would he like someone awful enough to be a Professional Meanie?

"I can't believe it," declared Marsha. She glared at Amber as if she wanted evidence. "Does Tommy like her back?"

Amber laughed. "Peally is in love with him, but

he doesn't like her anymore. I think . . . I mean, they did like each other once, about two summers ago."

Marsha leaned forward. Gossip always perked her up.

"Was Peally nice then?"

Amber shrugged, rolling her eyes up to the ceiling to think some more.

"I don't think so. But she was younger, so she wasn't into serious meanness like she is now."

Marsha slapped her hand down on the wooden table.

"Well, I'm glad Tommy dumped her. I hope he did it in front of the whole camp." Marsha grinned as she looked around the table.

Amber shook her head. "He wouldn't do that. Tommy is really a nice guy. He wouldn't even realize someone was being mean!"

The four of them nodded, silent in admiration.

"Well, who *does* he like?" asked Sarah.

"I don't know. Peally is kind of a shield. Every time Tommy is extra nice to someone, Peally steps in between them. I don't know what she says to them." Amber paused and tapped her fingers on the table. "Because, unfortunately, Tommy has never picked me to be his special friend . . . but whatever Peally says, it must be scary. The next thing you know, the girl is snubbing Tommy. No wonder he ends up taking Peally to the banquet every year."

"No," moaned Marsha. "He's too beautiful for that . . . that. . . ."

"Meanie." Amber laughed. "Every year we all sit around and try to think of the worst name we could call her. But the one that really fits is Meanie."

They all started to giggle. "We called her a Meanie, too," admitted Collette. She laughed, then felt her neck grow warm with guilt.

Meanie was what Stevie called Jeff when Jeff refused to let him play basketball with his friends.

Collette knew it wasn't nice to call people names. It was unkind, and it hurt other people's feelings.

But deep down in her heart Collette knew that a Meanie was exactly what Peally really was.

Chapter Five

Mr. Harrison, the camp director, was sitting on the steps of cabin seven when the girls walked back after dinner. He took his cap off and wiped his forehead with a huge checked handkerchief.

"Girls, I'm afraid your counselor still isn't here. She called to say she was having trouble with her van. So tonight and tomorrow I am assigning Sandy Smith to sleep in with you. She's a senior camper and has been up here quite a few years. She's moving her stuff up now, so have a good night. You will meet your counselor, Diane, on Tuesday."

With a final wave of his clipboard he walked down the path toward camp.

"Let's get organized," suggested Collette. She opened the screen door, swatting at the mosquitoes swarming around the bulbs on the porch.

"Isn't this fun?" Marsha asked. She twirled around the cabin. "I'm glad this cabin is ours."

Collette unrolled her sleeping bag on top of her bunk bed and nodded her head. Except for the trouble with Peally, Calvary Camp was absolutely perfect.

By the time Sandy Smith walked in, the girls had fixed their beds and hung up towels and robes.

"Hi, girls. I guess I'm just in time to walk you down to the marshmallow roast."

Sandy walked around and shook each of their hands, smiling like she was happy to be allowed to be their temporary counselor.

The four of them sang songs all the way down to the lake. It was so crowded and dark, Collette didn't even have time to worry about Peally and her friends trying to make trouble.

When they got there, Marsha snapped off a couple of twigs from a maple tree and handed one to

Collette. "I hope we tell ghost stories after the marshmallow roasting. I would love to be scared to death out here in the wilderness."

Sarah nudged Collette with her elbow. "Well, I'm getting scared right now. Look who's walking over to us."

Collette looked up to see Peally and her two friends strutting over. With the huge bonfire behind them, they looked like monsters emerging from a dragon's pit.

Sarah stabbed another marshmallow on the end of her stick and took a step closer to Collette.

"Just ignore them," instructed Collette softly. "They won't bother us."

When Peally was about four feet away from Collette and the girls, she stopped, put her hand on her hip, and gave a slow, mean smile.

"Well, the little rug rats are getting their marshmallows all ready," said Peally.

Right away Peally's two friends laughed as if Peally were a stand-up comic.

"Make sure you don't get too close to the big, bad fire, girls," Peally continued.

Collette added another marshmallow to her

stick, refusing to look up at Peally. Sometimes it was a lot better just to ignore a bully. A one-sided fight never lasted as long.

After a few quiet minutes Peally and her friends walked on, laughing and talking about how awful it was that rug rats were allowed to stay up this late.

"Boy, does she make me mad!" Marsha popped a white marshmallow into her mouth.

"She'll get tired of making fun of us if we just ignore it," said Collette.

Sarah and Marsha laughed. "That sounds like something you would find in a fortune cookie, Collette," said Sarah.

As the girls got closer to the fire, Collette could see Roger and his friends. She smiled as she watched Roger pretend he was going to swallow a flaming marshmallow.

"Don't eat too many, Collette."

Collette gripped her stick so tightly it snapped in two, and her marshmallow fell into the dirt. Tommy Hansley was standing two inches away from her. His blond hair was reflecting the light from the fire.

Tommy bent down and studied Collette's dirty marshmallow. He smiled and handed her his stick, crowned with three marshmallows.

"Here, Butterfingers! This might taste a little better."

Tommy nodded to all three girls and walked off toward Roger and the noisy boys. Collette held onto the stick as if it were the stem of a red, red rose.

"Well," asked Marsha, "are you going to roast it, or are you going to press it in your diary, Collette?"

Collette started to laugh as hard as Sarah.

"I'm just not hungry right now," she said, putting the stick down on the bench. "I'll roast it a little later."

"Sure," teased Sarah. "We'll all be waiting for that, Miss Butterfingers."

Collette looked out across the fire at the laughing boys, then up at the full, bright moon. She shivered in the cool night air.

"Let's tell Sandy we're going back to the cabin," suggested Collette. "I mean, it's late and it is getting cold."

Sarah flung her arm around Collette's shoulders and poked her in the side.

"Yeah, and you do need time to write another five or six pages in your diary, right, Collette?"

The three girls laughed the rest of the way up the path to their cabin.

Chapter Six

Monday morning

Dear Diary,

Roger and Tommy are getting to be good friends. Tommy says Roger is funny and that's great in a friend. Roger said that if Tommy weren't so good looking, he would be all right. They both ate breakfast with Marsha, Sarah, and me! I could hardly swallow. I was so happy!

Monday afternoon

Dear Diary,

Tommy is in my craft class. He said I was nice to make Stevie a headband. He asked if I could make him one, too. (I think he was joking?????) I read my notes from Laura, Jeff, and Stevie. They were funny. Laura said I was the best sister in the world. The boys didn't say that (of course!!) But Jeff taped his second favorite baseball card to his note for me to borrow, and Stevie said he would not go into my room and mess it up while I was gone.

Monday afternoon (again!!)

Dear Diary,

I know I already wrote... two hours ago. But Marsha said she heard someone by the sinks saying that she heard that Tommy Hansley thinks I am VERY *nice*. Marsha said the girl sounded really mad about the whole thing. Well... I have to get back for dinner. I hope Roger and Tommy want to sit at our table

again. Boy are they funny!
P.S. I think Tommy Hansley is NICE, too.

Monday

Dear Collette's Diary,
This is Sarah. Collette said I could write in you since she no longer lets me *read* you. Ha-Ha. I wonder why.... But since she is my best friend, I will forgive her. Ha-Ha. Collette is having fun up here. We have lots of classes, like crafts and horseback riding. I think

that is so we won't get in trouble. Ha-Ha. Anyway, I hope Collette reads this and lets me read her diary one day when she doesn't have a crush on Tommy Hansley. (Collette, don't be mad at me saying that because it's true and you know it!!!)

Monday night

Dear Diary,

Dinner was boring. Really sat with Tommy. I don't

know where Roger was. Peally laughed extra loud the whole dinner, so everyone would know how much fun she was having. She even pretended she was freezing to death, and Tommy gave her his sweatshirt to wear. It wasn't a bit cold in the dining room, either. I pretended that I didn't see, and I didn't say one mean thing about Peally. Being jealous is hard. It makes you want to say mean things. That's why I'm glad I have you, Diary. I can lock your mouth with a key (ha-ha). We are finally going to meet our counselor tomorrow. I hope she is as nice as Sandy. Boy, was she fun!

P.S.
We are having a softball game tomorrow. I have a good feeling that something wonderful is going to happen.

Chapter Seven

"I hope our new counselor lets us talk after lights out," said Collette. She broke off a twig and snapped it into little pieces. It was Tuesday, and they had just said good-bye to Sandy at lunch.

"Me, too," said Sarah. "That's the nicest part of the day."

Marsha laughed and tickled Collette under the chin with a wildflower. "Well, almost. I think Collette enjoys writing in her diary the most."

Sarah grabbed Marsha's arm and laughed. "No, it's being with Tommy so she has something to write about, Marsha."

"Stop it," Collette tried to sound mad, but it didn't work. Sarah and Marsha were having so much fun teasing her about Tommy. It was okay, though. It was like all three of them were sharing the crush on Tommy Hansley.

"Hey, look at that blonde leaning against that huge van," giggled Marsha. "Do you think she's Diane?"

Sarah groaned. "Gosh, that isn't a van. It's some sort of . . . of mobile home or trailer."

Diane looked up and waved the girls down the path.

"Are you cabin seven?"

"Yes," they called back. "Are you Diane?"

Diane made a slight bow.

Collette grinned back at Diane. She seemed nice and funny. Maybe Diane would be even more fun than Sandy. Camp was full of surprises, and so far, most of them had been great!

As soon as the girls sat down on the grass, Diane cleared her throat a couple of times and began. "Listen up, girls. I'm sorry about being late, but this mobile home is pretty bad on the road. I had a few flat tires, then I ran out of gas. . . ." Diane sighed and ran her fingers through her hair. "It took me forever to get here, and now that I'm here

I don't know why I bothered to come."

Collette and Sarah looked at each other with raised eyebrows. It sounded as if Diane didn't want to be at Calvary Camp.

"To tell you the truth, kids, this is my third year here, and I'm burned out."

Collette tried not to look disappointed. Burned out? Did that mean Diane would not want lots of fireside chats and long walks filled with great camp stories?

Collette looked at Diane's white linen shorts and pink silk blouse. She looked like she would rather be sipping iced tea next to a country club pool.

"We're not that much trouble," offered Sarah.

Collette nodded, wishing Diane would at least *try* to like being their counselor.

Diane took her time unwrapping a piece of gum and bending it into a neat square before popping it into her mouth.

"When I was your age, I was sick of my counselor hounding me all the time." Diane smiled down at the girls. "So I am going to cut you a break and *not* be around so much." She lowered her voice and glanced once over her shoulder. "I may spend my nights in the van here, since it cost me a small fortune, and it has a fan."

Collette almost laughed. "But aren't you supposed to sleep in our cabin and . . . kind of chaperone us?"

"And protect us!" added Marsha quickly.

Diane nodded.

"Ordinarily, yes, but the thing is, I am offering you girls much more freedom than the other cabins. Cabin seven is set off by itself, so it's already kind of . . . well, protected and . . ." Diane shrugged her shoulders, "I'll be with you guys during the day. I mean, I don't have to hold your hands while you sleep, do I?"

The girls giggled.

Diane clapped her hands together and turned to yank open her van door. "Let's celebrate with a cold can of soda. I have a refrigerator in here, so feel free to come in any time and help yourself!"

Marsha giggled and grabbed onto Collette's and Sarah's arms.

Collette squeezed back and tried to look happy. It worried her a little that they wouldn't have someone older with them at night. It wasn't because Collette was afraid of the dark, and she knew Calvary Camp didn't have robbers sneaking around.

Collette took a big sip of her root beer and looked out across the lake. She was being silly. She was so used to following rules and trying not to break any that she was just a little nervous.

"Come on, kiddoes," Diane called out, holding her can of orange soda high above her head. "Now, remember, my door here will always be open to you. . . ." Diane paused and took a long sip of soda. "Except when it's locked, which means I don't feel like having company."

Marsha covered her mouth with her hand, but Collette could hear the snicker anyway.

"Now remember," Diane continued as she headed down the path. "Keep our arrangements under your hat, or we'll have Mr. Harrison breathing down our necks, and none of us will enjoy our time here at Calvary. Let's get down to the game before they pick the teams."

"Boy, are we going to have fun," cried Marsha.

“It will be like a slumber party, except there won’t be a mother coming in at midnight to turn off the lights.”

“Lights go out at nine o’clock,” reminded Collette. “It was in the letter they sent home, remember?”

Collette bit her lip. She was getting a little nervous about all the rules being broken so quickly.

From the top of the hill, the girls looked down on crowds of kids assembled for the softball games.

Collette shook back her long blonde ponytail and felt a sudden burst of energy. She saw Roger and Tommy chasing each other across the field. This was going to be great. The field was big enough to have at least three games going at one time.

Collette reached out and grabbed Sarah’s arm. This was the part of camp she had been waiting for!

“Go on down and get assigned to a team,” suggested Diane. “I think I’ll go check out the other counselors.”

A few counselors were busy handing out colored scarves to be worn around the players' necks.

"Now you three girls go over there with the yellows," directed a short, square-looking fellow with red curly hair. He grinned at Collette as he handed her a scarf. "You look like you have a good arm there."

Marsha tied her scarf around her head, gypsy style. She put her hands on her hips and studied the field. She stamped her foot and frowned.

"Oh, phooey. Tommy is on the blue team, and we get silly old Roger!"

Collette was glad Roger was on their team. He was one of the best in their gym class at school. She peered over Marsha's head and tried to find Peally. Collette didn't want to be on the same team with her or her mean friends. Collette usually struck out, and it would be worse if her own team members booed her.

Over in the far field, near a grove of tall birch trees, sat Peally and her two friends.

"I guess they don't want to play," Collette said with a sigh of relief.

"Playing an all-American sport like softball might sap some of their meanness," declared

Marsha. She turned her head sharply away. "Come on, let's go down and talk to our team."

Sarah and Collette let Marsha run on ahead, her yellow scarf flapping in the breeze.

"Amber is on the blue team, too," said Collette. She waved at Amber and grinned when she waved back.

Sarah looked over her shoulder at Peally. "I hope Peally doesn't sneak in as a relief pitcher. She would try to hit us, for sure."

Collette shook her head. "Things will work out fine, Sarah. Haven't you ever seen those old camp movies where everyone hates each other in the beginning, and then by the end of the film they become best friends and promise to write. In one film, the enemies turned out to be related. . . ."

Sarah giggled. "Yeah, tomorrow morning we will wake up to find out that Peally is really your twin sister!"

Collette rolled her eyes. "We have enough kids at our house already. You can have Peally."

"Hey, let's get down here, ladies," Roger shouted from between cupped hands. "Let's play a little ball!"

"We might as well be back at Sacred Heart's gym," laughed Collette, as she and Sarah began to run down the hill. "All we need now is for Sister Mary Elizabeth to tell us to keep our voices down."

Marsha was hopping up and down in front of the coach, waving her yellow scarf.

"Let me play first, I'm good!" she kept shouting.

Sarah leaned over and whispered in Collette's ear.

"If Tommy or his cute friend Frank tag me out, I will never wash that spot again."

"You're nuts, Sarah!" said Collette, holding up her hand to be an outfielder. She smiled as she walked out to the field. Collette refused to act as excited as Marsha and Sarah about Tommy. Sure, he was nice-looking. In fact, he was cuter than any teenage movie star.

But he might as well *be* a movie star. He was just as unreachable. Even if he did notice a girl from camp, Peally seemed to have staked her claim to him. And she was determined to guard what she thought should be hers.

The blue team was up first. Tommy hit a home run, and Frank and Amber got on base. But then

Roger caught three fly balls to right field.

The yellow team ran back to home plate, cheering for Roger.

Marsha was up first. Even though she spent half the time arranging and rearranging her yellow scarf, she managed a good hit and got to second base.

Collette and Sarah laughed and clapped.

"Way to go, Cessano!" shouted Roger.

Marsha clapped for herself, curtsying and bowing from second base. She turned and waved to Tommy playing first.

"Bring me home, Roger!" Marsha yelled.

Roger picked up the bat and swung it back and forth. "Coming, dear!"

Collette laughed from the bench. Having Roger up at camp was nice. He had so much energy, and he used it all trying to be so funny.

Roger grabbed his yellow scarf and dusted off home plate. Then he jabbed it back in his pocket and swung at the first ball.

"Wait for your pitch, dummy!" Marsha screamed, shoving both hands on her hips.

"Yes, dear!"

Roger waited as the next ball sailed past, too far to the left. "Good eye!" shouted Marsha before she bent over in position.

"Bring me home, Roger! Hit a double!"

When Roger swung for the third time, he cracked the ball far off over third. It bounced once before it rolled down over the hill.

Roger held out his scarf as he raced around the bases. Marsha met him at home plate and pounded him on the back.

By the end of the third inning, yellow was ahead by four.

It started to cloud up at the top of the fifth inning, turning to a sprinkle by the bottom of the sixth. Collette was up at bat. She took a practice swing, then held out a hand to see how fast the drops were falling.

"Want to quit?" asked the red-haired fellow. He asked the question but he shook his head no. You could tell he was the type who was probably born outside in the middle of a snowstorm and would die by falling off a mountain when he was a hundred and four.

"Lightning!" shouted Diane from under her

large golfing umbrella. "Time to go in, girls."

Collette was glad Diane had suggested it, although she wasn't quite sure if Diane did it out of concern for her girls, or because she wanted to watch TV inside her mobile home.

"I'll catch you guys later. I'm going to eat in my van tonight," Diane shouted as she ran off.

"What a great game!" laughed Amber, waving her blue scarf. "You guys are really fast!"

"You, too. Boy, that was fun," said Sarah. Her face was streaked with mud from sliding into second base. "I hope we will all be on the same team tomorrow."

"Did you see that catch I made at third?" asked Marsha. Her scarf was now tied around her neck. "I hope we can play tomorrow, too. I am dying to play on Tommy's team. I wonder how I should wear this scarf tomorrow."

Amber reached out and shook Marsha. "Over your mouth, Marsha!"

After eating, the girls said good-bye to Amber at the fork and headed up the pine-needled path to cabin seven. It felt soft underfoot and smelled great, surrounded by the tall pines.

"Amber is nice," said Collette. "I told her we would pick her up at her cabin for breakfast tomorrow."

"Yeah, maybe we can all sign up for the same cabin next year," Marsha said. She pointed to cabin seven up ahead, looking small and welcoming in the dusk. "Now aren't you guys glad we are in this little cabin, just the three of us, off by ourselves?" Marsha sounded proud all over again that it had been her idea. "Total privacy!"

Collette nodded along with Sarah. The cabin did look special. It had been worth all the trouble to stake their claim.

It wasn't until they were by the front porch, closer to the large yellow bug light, that they skidded to a stop.

The entire front porch was decorated with their underwear! Panties and socks dangled everywhere. Even the bra Marsha hoped to wear one day was stretched across the screen door. Taped to the center was a little sign.

RUG RATS
ARE TOO
LITTLE
TO WEAR
BRAS!

"Holy cow," whispered Collette.

"Look at this!" shouted Marsha. She grabbed her bra from the door and looked around her with an angry stare. "My mother bought this at Trillium — the most expensive lingerie shop in town. How dare they even touch it!"

Sarah leaned against the wooden railing, shaking her head.

"We'd better go get Diane. Peally had to be the

one who did it. She didn't play softball with the rest of us. She snuck up here to raid our cabin."

"Let's get Diane is right," snapped Marsha, snatching up her bra and waving it in the air like Exhibit A.

"Yeah, come on. Diane will talk to Peally and settle this," said Collette, beginning to feel that things would be fixed.

It wasn't until they were at the end of the path that Collette stopped, reaching out to grab Marsha and Sarah by the arms. How could they go to their counselor for help?

Diane had never told them where she had parked her mobile home.

Chapter Eight

Back in the cabin, Collette's hand shook as she swept the cabin with the flashlight's soft white light.

"I sure wish my mom had let me pack a hunting knife," muttered Marsha. "We could use a little protection right now. The only weapons we have are three tennis rackets and a large can of bug spray."

Collette laughed. She didn't like the idea of her underwear being hung all over the front porch, but now that she knew no one was hiding in the cabin, she didn't think they were in any danger.

Besides, she had checked, and her diary and

key had not been touched. Nothing had been stolen.

"Well, no one is here so let's go to bed," Sarah said with a huge yawn. "When Diane comes up we can tell her, and she can report it, or whatever you do."

"Who knows where Diane is?" Marsha complained. "We need protection now. Maybe our underwear was a warning, and they are coming back to do something terrible to us."

Sarah and Collette started to laugh.

Marsha picked up her tennis racket and gave an experimental swing toward the screen door.

"Oh, go to sleep, both of you. I found this cabin all by myself, I guess I can guard it all by myself."

"Diane will be by real soon," Collette said. She stretched both arms over her head. She knew Marsha was feeling sorry for herself and wanted Sarah and Collette to beg her to go to sleep, offering to take turns guarding the cabin. "She promised she would check in with us."

The softball game had made Collette very tired. She lifted the lid of her trunk and pulled out her nightgown and a pair of clean socks, refolding a few shirts that Peally and her friends had mussed up while riffling through the cabin.

If mean old Peally wanted to sneak around outside the cabin, let her.

Collette turned off the flashlight and got under the covers. The bed felt cold and hard and didn't smell of fabric softener or bath soap. In fact, it didn't smell like anything from home. She turned her head to the other side, looking for a more comfortable spot. Her whole bed smelled like wet mud. She sat up, sniffing the air. It smelled like wet mud and. . . .

Across the room, Collette could see Sarah, sitting up in her bed and sniffing.

"Collette," Sarah called out. "Does your bed smell like . . . wet rags? It smells like the playground after a storm. Puddles — and mud and — "

"What?" cried Marsha, jumping from her post by the window. "You mean when *worms* are all over the place? Turn on the lights!"

Once the lights were on, both girls kicked off their covers and searched. Nothing was wrong with the sheets. It wasn't until Collette lifted her pillow that she saw the worms. There must have been twenty of them. Some were already squashed, parts of them wiggling in the air like angry snakes.

"Gross me out!" shrieked Marsha. She bolted to her own pillow. Her eyes bugged out. *"Disgusting."*

"What are we going to do with . . . with these worms?" asked Collette. She wasn't about to touch them. She knew worms didn't bite, but they were awfully slimy, especially the squashed ones.

Sarah let out a whimper, then a sob. It only took five seconds before she was crying her head off.

"I just want to go home," she wailed. "Camp was supposed to be fun! This whole night has been terrible!"

"Oh, Sarah! Don't cry." Collette hurried over. "We can all go home in the morning if things don't get better."

"Quitters," Marsha snapped angrily. She was trying to scoop the worm bits onto her tennis racket. As soon as she got a racket full, parts of them fell through the netting. "I'm not going to let that mean Peally scare me out of town!"

"Marsha, watch what you're doing," cried Collette. "You are dropping worm bits on the floor." Collette shivered and hopped on top of her trunk. "Oh, this is awful. I'm going to tell my dad to sue them all. They should go to jail for breaking and . . . and worming!"

Sarah looked up and giggled. "Breaking and worming? We'd better save the evidence then. Marsha, where is your bra? We'll have to take it into court."

Marsha whacked her racket down on the floor. "Wait till my parents hear about this. Maybe now they will send me to fancy camps with air-conditioned cabins, and guards to keep kids like Peally out."

Sarah nodded. "I can't believe Peally and her awful friends. Why are they devoting their time at camp to making our lives miserable? I mean, what's the big deal about this cabin? Is there gold buried underneath the floors?"

Collette raised her eyebrows, hopeful. "Would be nice. . . ."

"Wait a minute, wait a minute, here!" Marsha

dropped her racket, stepping over the worms to march to Collette.

"Sarah may have solved the case of the cabin, Collette. There has to be something in this cabin that Peally wants." Marsha rubbed her chin as she looked around the cabin.

"But why didn't they just take whatever they wanted when they were here?" Collette asked. "While we were playing baseball they took the time to trim our porch with underwear. They could have taken what they wanted then."

Marsha sat down on the bed, shoving her bangs up, then yanking them down. "Good point, Collette. Whatever they want is too big for them to carry off. Let's think about that . . . let's just think about how their mean little minds would work."

Collette looked up at Sarah and grinned. Marsha blossomed every time she took charge. Since she didn't have to look after any younger brothers or sisters, she made sure she looked after her friends.

"What is so special about cabin seven. . . ?" said

Marsha slowly. "It has a red door, but that wouldn't make Peally so crazy. . . ."

The three girls looked around the cabin. One set of bunk beds over by the far wall. Another by the window. One fold-out cot shoved in the closet. One large dresser by the door and a tiny wooden desk with a matching bright blue chair.

"I sure don't see any painting or vase worth a million bucks," Sarah said finally. She stretched up both arms and yawned. "I am too tired to even think about it anymore. Let's just go to sleep and worry about it in the morning."

"Wait a minute," said Collette. "Maybe there is a map or some secret messages taped in an envelope underneath the dresser drawers. They do that a lot in the mystery movies."

"A map to what?" asked Marsha. She frowned and shook her head.

Outside, a piercing whistle cut through the stillness.

Collette reached up and turned off the light. The three girls sat in silence, waiting.

"Do you think that was Peally?" asked Marsha in a hoarse whisper. "Maybe she's coming back."

"No. She only does things while we're gone. Come on, let's get our sleeping bags out and put them on the floor, away from the worms."

"I need a pillow," wailed Marsha. "If I sleep without a pillow I get terrible headaches."

"Oh Marsha . . ." Collette tried not to sound too mad. Here she was, trying to get everyone settled, and Marsha was still expecting hotel service.

"Roll up your sweatshirt, Marsha," Sarah suggested. She unrolled her sleeping bag and crawled inside. "Boy, am I ever tired. I thought camp was supposed to be relaxing."

"Migraine headaches run in my family," Marsha grumbled as she thunked her sweatshirt down. "Boy, oh, boy, will my parents be mad. If this cabin had a phone like it should, I would call them and tell them to — "

"Good night, Marsha!" Collette and Sarah both said.

The cabin was quiet. Collette rolled over and smiled. Hearing Marsha complain wasn't so bad. It almost sounded like home. And anyway, things would seem better in the morning. Birds would be singing, sunlight shining through the screens.

Maybe she could catch Tommy down by the lake and ask him to teach her how to fish. Amber said Tommy had won special fishing awards all across the state.

Jeff and Stevie would just about die laughing if Collette could bring home a snapshot of a big trout on the end of her line.

Collette flipped to her other side, giving a low groan as the tension left her legs. Sleeping on the floor wasn't so bad. And Peally and her friends would get tired of harrassing them if they just ignored the worm raid.

Tomorrow Marsha, Sarah, and Collette would just walk into the dining hall, laughing and happy as clams. They would have a fun breakfast and act like they had had hours and hours of relaxing sleep.

Maybe Collette would even nod her head and grin as she walked past Peally's table, letting her know Collette was a veteran camper and used to silly pranks.

Veteran campers *expected* pranks. It was part of camp life.

Collette smiled and stretched out both arms,

giving a huge yawn. Day three was over, and she had made it. Tomorrow was Wednesday, and she had fishing with Tommy to look forward to and. . . .

It wasn't until Collette yawned again, stretching out her toes and arms, that she felt the heavy, cool tube slither across her wrists.

Only it wasn't a tube. It was alive!

"Snakes!" cried Collette, leaping up as fast as she could.

She was screaming so loudly herself that she didn't know exactly when Marsha and Sarah started.

Chapter Nine

Early Wednesday morning, Diane was scowling at Collette, Marsha, and Sarah from the other side of Mr. Harrison's large oak desk.

Collette stared back and refused to feel the least bit guilty.

After all, she hadn't reported that Diane was off in a mobile home, eating chips and dip and watching the late show while worms and snakes crawled all over cabin seven.

Collette never meant to get anyone in trouble, but she couldn't help her scream. The worms hadn't bothered her that much, but a fat snake sliding all over her wrists. . . .

Besides, it was Marsha screaming like her hair

was on fire that really brought everyone running. She was convinced the snake had crawled down her pajamas.

"Here is your paycheck for one day's work, Diane," said Mr. Harrison. He wasn't yelling, but his voice was almost dripping with disappointment.

Diane took it without saying thank you.

Mr. Harrison held out his hand and waited until Diane took off her whistle and put it into his waiting palm.

"Diane, you are very lucky nothing more serious happened to these young ladies," he continued.

"Serious?" Diane gave a short laugh. "Mr. Harrison, I don't call a few dead worms and a water snake serious. . . ." Diane held up both hands like a traffic cop. "But, hey, listen . . . I'm out of here, and that's fine with me."

As Diane turned to go, Marsha stepped forward. "My parents' attorney will be in touch, Diane."

Diane narrowed her eyes and shot Marsha a nasty look before she marched out the door, slamming it behind her.

"Girls, I wish you'd told me about Diane not

being in your cabin before we had this unfortunate situation." Mr. Harrison stood, his bald head almost hitting the ceiling of the small office. "Luckily we heard the screaming and came running."

Marsha smiled smugly. "I thought screaming was the quickest way to alert you, Mr. Harrison."

Sarah and Collette glanced at each other, then down at the floor so they wouldn't start laughing all over again. Marsha was so funny without even knowing it. Her scream hadn't been a planned alert. It had been an explosion of nerves. The camp nurse had almost had to give Marsha a sedative to quiet her down.

"Edith-Ann Waintill will be your new counselor. I just talked to her last night on the phone, and she should be here any time now. She'll catch up with you during the afternoon. And I can assure you three that you will have constant supervision from now on."

Mr. Harrison beamed at the girls, hitching up his pants and nodding as though he had just tied up their camp week in a neat little package.

Collette gave a slight nod back. No one had

squealed on Peally and her band of Meanies. They didn't have any real proof to hand Mr. Harrison, and if Peally were questioned and set free, she would be madder than ever.

Revenge was something Peally seemed to take very seriously.

"Now go out there and enjoy this beautiful day!" ordered Mr. Harrison with a hearty laugh. "Nothing like a Wednesday morning at Calvary Camp!"

"Thank you, Mr. Harrison," they chanted as they raced outside and down the wooden steps.

"Enjoy your day . . ." repeated Marsha. "I wish we could have dusted the cabin for fingerprints. Then we could have sent Peally up the river for breaking and entering, terrorist threats, and . . . and being a pain in the neck."

"I guess we aren't doing such a great job of making friends up here," Collette said. "We'd better make sure Diane doesn't try to run us over with her mobile home."

The girls laughed. Marsha reached out and linked arms with Collette and Sarah.

"We're friends with each other, and that's enough. At least we can *trust* each other. Boy, oh boy, it gives me the creeps to know how few people we can trust at this crummy camp."

"We can trust Amber," Sarah reminded her. "Gosh, we forgot to pick her up for breakfast because of the meeting with Mr. Harrison. . . ."

"Wait till she hears what happened," Marsha giggled.

Collette smiled, glad that the sun was out and she was with Sarah and Marsha. Camp had been pretty wild so far, but it was still fun. And there was a lot more to come.

"We'd better get to swim class, or we'll have to do push-ups," said Collette. "I hope Roger wears those Hawaiian swim trunks again. He is so funny."

Marsha frowned. "Roger is weird. Besides, thanks to his big mouth, Peally is madder than ever. I think we should stay far away from Roger Friday until we leave camp."

"Roger's okay," said Sarah. "He didn't mean to make things worse. He was trying to help Collette, Marsha. I'm kind of glad someone from Sacred Heart is here."

Marsha broke free and shoved both hands into

her pockets. "Roger is trouble, trust me. The kid must have been born during an eclipse or something."

"I wonder what Edith-Ann will be like?" Collette laughed. "Her name makes her sound like someone who likes to read the encyclopedia for fun."

"Our counselor will be sleeping in our cabin, that's all we need her for," said Marsha. "Listen, girls, we still have plenty of days left at camp, and nothing is going to spoil them. I read that camp is something that stays with you till you drop dead, and I don't want bad memories, okay?"

"That's the spirit, Marsha," said Collette.

Marsha pushed back her hair and gave it a proud shake.

"I am a fun-loving person, and I want my camp memories to be as positive as they can be."

Sarah patted Marsha on the back and grinned at Collette. Collette giggled. Marsha could be a pain in the neck at times, but she did have such a huge zest for just about everything. That was the part of Marsha that was so terrific. The part that made up for a lot of the dumb things she said.

"So let's just go down to the lake, swim our test so we can get into the mermaid group, show everyone that we still have the cutest suits, and . . . and have fun!"

"Let's go!" laughed Collette.

The three girls ran down the dirt path to the dock. They could see row after row of camp sailboats and canoes.

Several of the sailboats were already far out on the lake. Collette noticed Peally and her thin friend getting into their canoe.

"Amber said the skinny one is named Louise," Marsha whispered. She gave a short, cold laugh. "Nobody in real life is named Louise."

Collette liked the name Louise. It was pretty and old-fashioned.

Sarah nudged Marsha. "Hey, my favorite aunt is named Louise."

Marsha waved her hand at Sarah. "Well, of course *aunts* are named Louise. Librarians can be Louises and probably a couple thousand piano teachers, too. But no *kid* in America is named Louise."

"You're nuts, Marsha!" Collette laughed. Marsha had so many theories about everything, and she thought they were all exactly true.

"Look how blue the water is!" cried Sarah. She pulled her sweatshirt off and stepped out of her shorts. "Like my new suit? I can hardly wait to jump in."

"Holy cow!" giggled Marsha. "Look at Roger's new bathing suit. Doesn't that kid have a mother?"

Roger was flying through the air to the lake in a pair of baggy, red polka-dot trunks. As soon as he hit the water, a loud whoop followed.

"Well girls, glad to see you finally made it down to the lake," called out the tall, curly haired counselor named Fred. "You're already fifteen minutes late, so hustle on down here and let me see if you can pass the test."

Fred waved the towel over his head. "Come on now, who wants to go first?"

Marsha raised her hand, waving it as if she were back in school.

"Fred, listen. I've had private swim lessons at my club since I was four. You know I can swim. Do I still have to take the swim test?"

Fred gave Marsha a slight bow. "Yes, my dear, you do. But I'll make sure we have a warm towel waiting for you when you get out."

Collette couldn't help but laugh.

"Get wet, girls, and we'll start in five minutes," Fred stated.

Collette sat down and lowered her toe into the water. "Boy, is this cold. Can't we wait until after lunch to take the swim test?"

Fred walked over, rubbing his chin. "You may have a point there, Collette. Let me see how cold the water is." He bent down and picked Collette up, tossing her over the side of the dock.

"How cold is it?" he hooted from the dock.

Collette's screams mixed with laughter as she plunged down into the chilly water. She pushed herself back up, sputtering and laughing at the same time. This was great! Everyone always got tossed into the lake in camp books.

Roger pulled his goggles down over his eyes and jumped feet first into the water.

"Geronimo!" he hooted.

Collette held up her hands as the lake water washed over her.

"You okay, Murphy?" he asked as he dog-paddled toward her.

Collette nodded, looking past Roger at Marsha and then Sarah as they were each tossed into the lake.

Roger dove under the water and grabbed onto Marsha's legs, pulling her under the water for a second time.

"Get away from me, Roger," Marsha gasped, waving both arms back and forth like a sprinkler.

"You're in shock, Marsha," shouted Roger. He put his arm under her chin and started to swim toward the dock. "Lie still and let me save you."

"Let go of me, Roger Friday!" sputtered Marsha.

Sarah swam up beside Collette and rolled her eyes. "Roger is really going to get it from Marsha one of these days."

As she treaded water, Collette nodded. "I noticed you got thrown in, too."

Sarah ducked her head back and smoothed her long reddish hair. "Some counselor named Nicky. Boy, was he cute!"

"Cuter than Tommy?"

It slipped out so fast, Collette didn't even have time to think about how it might sound.

Sarah cupped a handful of water and splashed it against Collette. "Well, Collette, *you* wouldn't think anyone was cuter than Tommy. I saw you scribbling away in your diary last night, and I don't think you were describing a marshmallow roast after dinner, or craft class."

"I was," laughed Collette. "Didn't you see that nice little Indian headband I started for Stevie? And then I wrote — "

Collette stopped. She couldn't lie to Sarah. It was true, half of her diary was already filled. It wasn't that so many wonderful things were happening with Tommy, because she had only known him for a few days. It was just that every time she even saw him she had so many wonderful feelings and thoughts to write about.

Collette felt herself blushing in the warm afternoon sun. Sunday night she had *slightly* exaggerated what had really happened at the marshmallow roast. But it was her diary, and exaggerating wasn't really lying. Not really. . . .

Sunday night

Dear Diary,

Tommy is so sweet. He gave me a present at the marshmallow roast. He even called me a cute little nickname. I wonder what nickname I could give him—Handsome! Mr. Muscle! ♡ ♡

"Yoo-hoo, Sarah to Collette. Wake up, please!" Sarah splashed Collette. "I bet you're thinking about that diary again. The diary you won't even let me read anymore!"

"It's nothing," Collette said slowly. The truth was, Collette did feel a little funny about not letting Sarah read her diary. Sarah had been her best friend since the third grade, and they just didn't keep secrets from each other. They used to trade diaries, sitting up in bed and giggling over each other's entries, stupid stuff about mean substitutes, gross school lunches, and embarrassing things boys said during class.

But this time the diary was different. She had already put so many different entries in since she had arrived at camp. Tommy was special. It was the first time in her life that Collette thought about someone even when she wasn't with them. Tommy Hansley was like a catchy jingle from a commercial — he kept popping into her head without warning. Collette had felt it the first time she saw him.

"Well, when can I read it?" asked Sarah. This time she really wanted to know.

"I don't know." Collette looked right at Sarah to let her know she was telling the truth. She didn't know. Each time she wrote in her diary she had no idea what was going to come out of her. All she knew for sure was that it would be about Tommy. And the more she wrote about him, the more confused Collette became.

Did she like Tommy Hansley because it gave

her something special to write about, or did she write about him because he was so special?

"Boy, you must have a giant crush on this guy, Collette. You've made him so top secret." Sarah looked serious and a little jealous. Neither one of them had ever liked a boy this much before.

Sarah had liked Petey Bennet last year, for a week. But Petey never knew about it, so it really didn't count.

"I don't know, Sarah. I mean, I'm not sure how this liking business is supposed to work."

"Collette, do you really . . . ?"

Collette shrugged, then laughed and dunked herself under the water.

"You're still blushing, Collette," Sarah laughed.

"Hey Messland, get over here, pronto!" shouted Fred. He waved her over with his clipboard. "Swim test time!"

Collette watched Sarah do her best breast stroke over. She was probably hoping Nicky or Frank were watching from the dock.

Collette dove back under the water, feeling free and very grown up. It was wonderful to be able to be in charge of herself. And only herself. She didn't have to watch her younger sister or make sure the boys didn't wrestle in the water.

Collette swam deeper, touching the sandy bottom with her fingertips. Making a graceful circle, she pushed herself up through the water, her hair straight behind her like a mermaid's.

Just then something grabbed tightly around her ankle, pulling her back so quickly she flung out both arms.

Were there snakes in the lake? Big snakes?

Next she felt two large hands around her waist, pushing her up so fast she burst through the crest of the water.

"Hi, Collette!"

Tommy twisted her around to face him. "I thought you were ready to come up for air."

With both hands, Collette wiped the water away from her eyes and shook back her hair. As she tried to smile she began to choke on the water.

"You okay?"

Collette nodded and opened her eyes. Tommy was less than a nose away from her face. She sucked her breath in so suddenly she started to choke all over again.

"Man overboard!" Roger shouted from the dock. He flung out a life preserver and jumped into the water after it.

"Here comes your personal bodyguard," said Tommy. He let go of Collette's waist and leaped backwards, both arms outstretched. "That kid is like your shadow."

Collette turned and watched Roger swimming furiously toward her, his bright bathing cap popping up and down like a buoy.

"Would you like to go fishing? Maybe you can meet me down by the dock tomorrow morning before breakfast," Tommy said. "At six, before old Roger the Dodger has a chance to wake up."

"Sure," Collette said quickly. She smiled and nodded her head up and down. "Sure. That sounds like fun."

"Am I in time?" sputtered Roger. He weakly plunked the life preserver around Collette's neck and sighed. "I thought I'd never make it, Collette."

"Roger, I wasn't drowning," Collette laughed. She ducked out from under the preserver and gave it a shove closer to Roger. "I was just having fun. Thanks, anyway."

Still smiling, she turned to say something to Tommy. But when she looked behind her, he was already swimming toward the dock. Swimming straight to the long shadow cast by Peally and her friends.

Chapter Ten

When the girls raced back to the cabin after swimming, they met Edith-Ann and her giant silver clipboard.

"I checked the cabin, girls, and I am pleased with the neatly made beds. You're Marsha, right? You left an open bag of cookies in there, so watch it or we will have seven ants in cabin seven!"

Edith-Ann threw back her head and laughed hard at her own joke.

"Seriously now," Edith-Ann continued, smiling broadly at each girl. "I think we'll make a good team. I knew it the minute you walked in here. You are fine material for Games Day tomorrow! I just know we will walk away with at least one trophy at the banquet on Friday."

"Edith-Ann, we are missing lunch," reminded Marsha. "Can we grab our tennis rackets and leave? We . . . we have to keep our strength up for Games Day."

Edith-Ann consulted her clipboard and nodded. "Yes, run off and fortify yourselves, girls. I will pick you up late this afternoon for a brisk two-mile walk up the mountain. Then we will have to get to bed early so we can slip in a quick mile jog before Games Day begins." Edith-Ann made a notation on her clipboard. "We can fit it in right before breakfast."

"Before breakfast?" Collette yelped. The only thing she wanted to do before breakfast tomorrow was to go down to the lake and meet Tommy Hansley.

She didn't want to hurt Edith-Ann's feelings, but she would much rather sit side by side on the dock with Tommy and listen to his fishing stories than run up the side of a mountain.

Edith-Ann was a nice counselor. Much more attentive than Diane, but she was taking her job seriously. Maybe a little too seriously. Games Day was like the Olympics to her.

She wanted to whip Marsha, Sarah, and Collette into shape so badly that she would probably insist on teaching them to rope cattle after lunch and swim to the island and back before dinner.

"Off you go, troops!" Edith-Ann cried as she opened wide the screen door. "Fortify, fuel up for all our activities."

The girls were silent as they filed past and down the wooden stairs. Edith-Ann's high-voltage energy seemed to have zapped theirs.

"Boy, that girl is worse than a parole officer," Marsha groaned. "She has a whole clipboard full of activities for us. She's going to be our shadow, whether we like it or not."

"At least she's bigger than Peally," Collette added.

Sarah pulled open the wooden doors leading to the dining room. "Well, if we eat fast, we can do something fun before horseback riding. We're due there at two."

Over lunch Collette just pushed her food

around the plate. She couldn't eat. She didn't feel sick, just — different. Nothing could get past the lump that had bubbled up from her heart.

"Look at her," giggled Sarah, nudging Marsha. "The girl is in love!"

Collette looked up, ready to protest. But as soon as she opened her mouth, she started to laugh.

"Tommy's nice, that's all."

"Sure, Collette," Marsha agreed. "So is Fred, the lifeguard, but you don't see Sarah and me writing ninety pages a day in a diary about him."

Sarah gave a theatrical sigh, patting Collette on the arm. "Enjoy it, Collette. We're just jealous."

Collette grinned back. Why should she try to pretend that Tommy wasn't the nicest boy she had ever met? He was so grown up, so much more understanding than any of the boys at Sacred Heart Elementary.

And the amazing part was, he liked her. He liked her more than Marsha or Sarah or a lot of really pretty girls at camp.

Taking a tiny lick of her pudding, Collette sighed. She could hardly wait to get up early the next morning and run down to the dock to meet Tommy. She hoped Edith-Ann would understand. She and Tommy would probably be the first two up at camp. Maybe the sky would still be pink, the sun halfway up in the —

"Hello again you three!" Edith-Ann sat heavily into a chair and rattled her clipboard on the table. "I've checked our itinerary, and our afternoon is set. Hurry with your lunches, now. The sooner we start working out for Games Day, the sooner we can picture that trophy sitting on top of the dresser in cabin seven."

"Edith-Ann, we have horseback riding this afternoon," began Sarah.

"And then we have to go over to the kiln to see if our pots are dry," added Collette.

"And besides, we don't have to spend every minute together, do we?" finished Marsha. "I mean, it seems like you want us to be together every minute of the day."

"I know," said Edith-Ann. She smiled and looked very proud. "Mr. Harrison asked me to be with you as much as possible, since Diane had not been with you at all."

Marsha grabbed her tray and stood up.

"Girls, you will thank me on Saturday, when you hold that trophy high as you ride off into the sunset!" Edith-Ann thought for a second and scribbled what she had just said onto her clipboard.

"I don't really care if I win a dinky trophy or not, Edith-Ann. I don't care about the mile race, the pass-the-baton relays or . . . or who can swim backwards the fastest. . . ."

"You don't *care*?" Edith-Ann bolted from her chair and scowled. "First of all, the trophy is not dinky, and second of all, I care, and I'm in charge of the cabin. Mr. Harrison took me away from a perfectly fine job of selling Avon for the summer, at the last minute, to come up here and be your counselor, so we *will* participate in Games Day, and we *will* win. Got that?"

Before anyone could say a word, Edith-Ann flung her whistle around her neck like a cape and stormed off.

"Golly . . ." whispered Sarah. "She sure wants that trophy. Maybe we'd better try to win some of the races for her."

Collette tossed her napkin onto her tray and

stood up. "Fine with me. Games Day is supposed to be fun." As she looked to the door, she slowly slid back down into her seat, her face bright red.

Marsha leaned closer to Collette. "What's wrong with you? Your face is on fire!"

Sarah twisted in her seat and watched as Tommy and his friends burst into the dining hall.

Collette looked down at her tray, searching for something to nibble on so she could stay a little bit longer. Maybe Tommy would stop by the table and mention their . . . their meeting tomorrow morning. Should she call it a date?

"Hey, Murphy!" Tommy said as he walked right over.

"Hi, Tommy!" said Marsha quickly. "You're lucky you got here in time. The ladies were starting to put away the food."

Tommy held up an arm and called to the head cafeteria worker, "Milly, don't you dare put anything away!"

Milly looked up and smiled when she saw it was Tommy.

"You hurry then, Mr. Hansley. I don't have special hours just for you."

Tommy looked back at Collette and grinned. "She's dating my uncle, so I'll get fed!"

"Not unless we hurry, Tommy!"

Collette felt as though someone had just socked her in the stomach. Peally had just come up from behind Tommy and put her hand on his shoulder.

"Come on, Tommy. I'm starving." Peally looked right at Collette and gave a sticky sweet smile. "We've been sailing for over an hour, and you know how hungry that makes me, Tommy."

Tommy reached out and pulled on Collette's ponytail before he moved away with Peally. The two started laughing and joined a noisy group moving through the line. You could tell they were all old friends, all part of a little group.

"Peally was sailing with Tommy," said Marsha. She said it right out loud, as if she were a newscaster.

Sarah reached over and put her hand on Collette's arm. Collette could barely feel it since her whole body was turning numb. Tommy had spent the rest of the morning with Peally. He'd probably had so much fun with her he would forget all about the next morning.

The next day at six Collette would be standing all alone on the dock under a perfect pink sky.

"You are much, much prettier than Peally," Marsha said quickly. "And you make straight A's, which is just as important as having long, long legs."

Collette looked at Marsha for a second before she started to laugh. She laughed so hard that soon Marsha and Sarah started.

"Why are we laughing?" asked Sarah as she tried to stop.

Collette shrugged, and the three started laughing harder than ever. Who needed perfect legs when you had A's in science and math?

From behind her Collette could hear Peally's loud, hard laugh. "Tommy Hansley, you bad thing!" she hooted.

Collette slowly picked up her tray and tried to keep her back as straight as possible. She wasn't going to let Peally or Tommy ruin her week at camp.

"Let's get out of here before Edith-Ann asks us to do a quick hundred push-ups," Sarah suggested. "If we're not here, we won't have to follow her crazy schedule."

Collette walked to the tray table and set down her tray. Riding would be fun, and she was getting pretty good at getting the horse to obey.

"Collette?"

Collette could smell Tommy's cocoa butter suntan lotion before she even turned around.

"Listen, I bought some bait after swimming. Instead of meeting me tomorrow morning, could you meet me after lunch today? Down by the dock, near the yellow benches? I want to show you my new fishing rod."

Collette glanced at Marsha and Sarah, both of whom shoved their hands in their pockets and looked in different corners of the room.

"Can I steal Collette away from you guys?" asked Tommy. "For a measley hour?"

Marsha nodded. "Sure, as long as she doesn't catch any fish and try to bring them back to the cabin."

Tommy laughed. "Maybe we can catch all the fish we'll need for the banquet. Hansley and Murphy catering!" He headed back to his table, then turned and gave Collette a wave. "See you soon, Collette!"

Collette turned away, not wanting to see Peally's angry face, or hear her loud laugh. She stepped out into the bright sunshine, hardly able to wait to get to the cabin and write everything down in her diary before she forgot it.

Collette smiled, already forming the sentences in her mind:

Dear Diary,
Tommy wants me to go fishing right away. He doesn't want to wait another minute. I think I am going to change into my yellow shirt. I think Peally may be mad, but she doesn't own Tommy Hansley. No one does!!!

Collette pulled open the screen door and paused, thinking. She didn't have to write down that Tommy and Peally ate lunch together, did she? Or that Tommy really did laugh a lot around Peally and her friends? None of that meant a thing. Peally and Tommy had gone to school together since kindergarten, just like Roger and Collette.

It didn't mean a thing. Nothing worth writing about.

Chapter Eleven

When Collette opened the door, the cabin was still cool, the only sunlight coming from around the blinds at the open back window.

Collette rolled up the green slat blinds, filling the room with sunlight. She turned and automatically closed the open window, looking around for the missing screen. Marsha or Sarah must have taken it out for some reason, forgetting about the thousands of mosquitoes just waiting to fly in.

She sat on her bed and reached underneath the springs for her diary key, sliding her hand around. Then she twisted off the bed and poked her head under.

She couldn't see the key dangling from the red

shoelace anywhere. Down on all fours, Collette stretched her arm out and swept the floor with a huge stroke.

As she sat up, she looked around the cabin. Sarah and Marsha wouldn't have taken the key. Marsha had acted huffy when Collette had refused to let her read it, but she wasn't the sneaky type. At times Marsha was too honest. Whatever she was feeling, she was glad to let you know.

Collette got up slowly and walked toward the heavy green dresser in the corner of the room. Maybe she had accidentally forgotten and left the key in the diary. She had been tired last night when she had finally finished writing.

Collette knelt and felt around the floor, her fingers flicking off cobwebs as she patted along.

"I really must have tossed it last night," Collette mumbled as she stretched out and extended her arm as far as it would go.

She wrinkled up her nose at the dusty, sour smell coming from the floorboards. Next time she would just tuck the diary under the dresser so it wouldn't require a search party.

After a final stretch, Collette stood, dusting herself off. Too bad Sarah wasn't here. She could use her help to move the dresser.

Collette pushed her hip against the dresser, inching it away from the wall. After four or five pushes, she stopped and peered behind the dresser. There was nothing but dustballs, and. . . .

And . . . what was that smeared on the wall?

Collette gripped the dresser, getting a fresh spurt of energy as she read more of the message. Using both hands, she shoved the dresser away from the wall. She bent down and studied a large red heart painted on the pale green wall.

In the center of the large heart was printed:

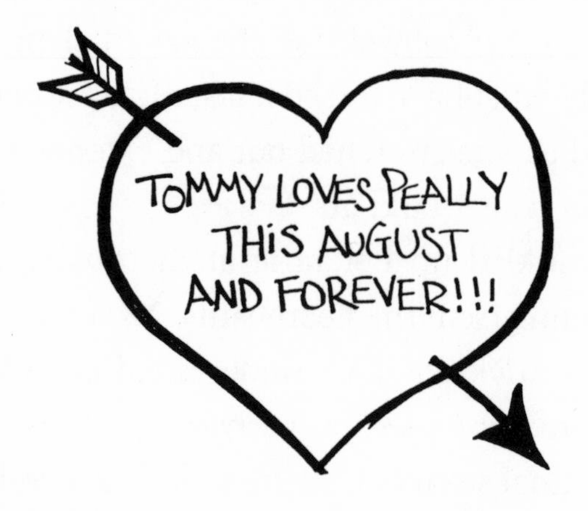

Her mouth open in disbelief, Collette read and reread the message before turning her back on it.

She glanced at the back window, half expecting Peally to be staring back in at her.

No wonder Peally wanted this cabin again this summer. A page of Peally's diary was painted right on the wall.

Remembering her own diary, Collette turned, shoving herself in between the dresser and the wall. She stooped and her hand brushed across the bare floor.

It wasn't there. The diary wasn't under the dresser at all!

Collette hurried across the cabin, lifting her pillow and top sheet in one swift shake. She remembered writing three whole pages last night.

She had slid the diary back under. She'd heard a soft *thunk* as it hit the wall behind the dresser.

The more she remembered, the worse she felt. She knew she had put the diary back last night. And she hadn't written anything in it today because she had been too busy with the swim test.

Collette looked down at the floor by the dresser. Several scrape marks had been etched into the wooden floor like giant windshield wiper marks. Lots of scrape marks.

A tiny spot in Collette's stomach started to burn. She hadn't been the only one moving the dresser. Someone else had been inside the cabin since last night looking for something.

Peally!

Angry tears burned Collette's eyes. Peally had marched right in, thinking she owned the cabin because Tommy had painted a red heart with her name on it.

Collette stared down at the heart. Did Peally come into the cabin to look at her heart, and then steal the diary? Or had she come to break into Collette's private things, and ended up finding the diary lying beneath the heart?

Collette leaned against the wall, covering her warm face with her hands. She wanted to go home, *right* now. She never wanted to meet anyone face to face who had read her diary. They had read her soul!

Page after page of her diary floated in front of her.

Dear Diary,
Tommy said he would keep an eye on me all week. What a cute bodyguard!!

Dear Diary,
At times I feel funny not letting Sarah read you. But I am not ready to share Tommy with anyone!! He's my secret.
? ? ?

Dear Diary,
Tommy said my hair always looks so great, even when it's wet!! He looks cute wet or dry. He is Calvary Camp's cutest guy! (Ha-Ha!)

Dear Diary-
Amber said Peally said that Tommy kissed her once. I don't believe it at all. Peally made it up!! At least I hope so!!

BANQUET

Dear Diary,
I am almost 100% sure Tommy will ask me to sit at his table for the banquet!! He asked me if I had made plans yet and then I think he winked at me—Oh well—more later!!!

Collette shuddered as the thoughts that had been locked in her diary surrounded her.

She wanted to go home. NOW!

She could start packing her trunk immediately, telling Edith-Ann that she was sick. Maybe poisoned by eating old potato salad. Her mother would rush up here and take her back to her house, where everything was noisy, crowded, and hectic, but safe.

The large heart on the wall seemed to be staring at Collette. One red unblinking eye glaring at her for invading cabin seven, Calvary Camp, and for liking Tommy Hansley.

Collette glared back, crossed her arms, and marched over to it, ready for the shoot-out. She studied the heart as though it were the enemy, reading it again and again.

"Wait a minute," Collette whispered, bending down closer.

Tommy didn't paint that! Tommy wouldn't sneak into a girls' cabin with a can of red paint and mark up a wall, just to make Peally happy.

Peally painted it. No boy, not even Tommy, would bother making a heart that perfect. They wouldn't ever remember to put the arrow through it.

Maybe Tommy didn't even know the heart was in cabin seven.

Collette looked at the back window, a gaping hole without the screen. Peally's laughter seemed to rise and float through it, laughing and glad that Collette had discovered her diary was missing.

Collette shoved the dresser back against the wall with four fierce thrusts. She wasn't ready to pack her trunk and leave camp.

Not yet. Not until she got her diary back.

Chapter Twelve

Collette took a deep breath as she sat on the yellow bench by the lake. She wasn't going to mention the missing diary to Tommy. How could she? He would just say, "Oh, forget it. Buy yourself a new one."

Boys didn't understand about diaries, how private they were. Anyway, how could she tell him that the diary had been filled with page after page of Tommy stuff?

Collette bent down and retied her tennis shoe for the fifth time. She had been sitting on the bench for a long time. It was almost time for riding lessons. How much food could Tommy eat?

From the top of the hill she heard shouting. For

a second Collette was afraid to look up, sure she would see Peally and her friends following Tommy down the dirt path to the lake.

"Sorry I'm late!" Tommy sat down on the bench next to Collette and put a can of worms between them.

"I had to run back and get my fishing rod out of hiding."

"Hiding?"

Tommy laughed. "Hey, this baby cost a bundle. I can't just prop it outside my cabin, can I?"

Collette looked at the fiery-red fishing rod. It was pretty, for a fishing rod. She could tell by the way Tommy was holding it that he thought it was beautiful. "I worked weekends in my dad's grocery store to buy this. Want to hold it?"

Collette almost said no, but she held out her hand for the rod. If Tommy loved to fish so much, it must be wonderful.

"I've never fished before. Is it hard?"

Tommy shook his head. "No. Casting is a little tough, but I'll show you a few tricks. Ready?"

Collette stood up and carried the rod while Tommy gathered up his bait and towels. "Wait a second, Collette. I almost forgot. You need this before we start our first lesson."

Collette stopped, hoping it wasn't a thick manual she had to read about fishing. Or a huge worm.

Tommy came up beside her and put a worn-looking cap on Collette's head. On each side dangled a feathery hook.

"Can't catch a fish big enough to keep unless you look the part."

Reaching up, Collette touched the cap. It felt soft and smooth, like an old sweatshirt.

"Watch out for the hooks," Tommy said, pulling Collette's hand away. "If you're a good fisherman, er, girl, you can keep the cap. My granddad gave it to me when I started out."

Collette gripped the fishing rod more tightly. Her hand almost shook, she felt so honored that Tommy had given her such a nice present. It was much nicer than the marshmallow stick Sunday night. It was something she could keep . . . forever!

By the time Tommy had explained every section of the rod and made Collette hold a horrible-looking worm, the sun was hot. Sweat trickled down her neck, but Collette didn't even think about suggesting a cool dip in the lake. It was much too nice sitting on the dock, side by side with Tommy. If anyone from camp were to look down and see the two of them, they would think they had to be good friends.

"That Indian headband you made Stevie is cool," said Tommy. He brought the rod back over his right shoulder and flung the line forward in a smooth arc. "Have you started mine yet?"

Collette laughed. "Would you wear it?"

"Yeah, sure," Tommy tried not to smile, but Collette could see one side of his mouth turn up. "I just might wear it to the banquet Friday night if you get it done in time."

"Okay." Collette looked out across the lake. Tommy was probably kidding about wearing the headband, but she would make it, even if she had to stay up all night. Sometimes it was hard to tell when boys were teasing. She didn't want to take any chances on disappointing him.

"What are you two doing?"

Collette jumped and automatically reached up for her hat. Roger wiggled in between them and sat down. He pulled off each huge tennis shoe and dangled his feet in the water.

"So, what's up, guys?" he asked. "What are we doing this afternoon?"

"We're fishing, Rog, so don't look into the water and scare them away."

"Ha-ha," Roger said. He poked Collette in the side with his elbow. "You look like a real fisherman in that hat, Collette."

"She is, Roger. Watch her cast off. She's a fast learner."

Tommy held out his rod. "Go on, Collette. Reel it in and cast off."

Collette shook her head. She didn't think she was ready to go public with her fishing. Every time she had tried to cast, the hook only went a few yards. Then Tommy had to reel it in and let her start over.

"Go on. You have to try or I take back the hat."

Roger's face looked strange for a second. He stared at Tommy, then at the hat, and finally at Collette.

Collette took the rod and stood up. Maybe if she were up higher, it would go further.

"There you are!"

Collette jumped, expecting to see Edith-Ann, clipboard in hand, ready to drag her off for Games Day exercises.

Instead, there Peally stood, one hand on her hip. She glared at Collette before she gave a big smile to Tommy and Roger.

"Tommy, you said you would help me untangle the nets for volleyball tonight. You promised."

Tommy shrugged, squinting against the sun. "Yeah, well, it doesn't have to be right now, does it?"

Peally shook back her mane of blonde hair and sighed.

"Well, I did want to get things set up so we could start playing right after dinner. Don't forget our annual Calvary Volleyball Tournament."

Peally waited a long moment before she added. "We do this with the same group of kids each year. Sorry we can't ask you two newcomers to join us."

Tommy stood up and readjusted the rod in Collette's hand. "Don't try to choke it to death, Collette. Relax that grip."

Peally looked wounded. "I thought no one was

allowed to touch that rod, Tommy. Especially someone like Collette, who obviously doesn't know a thing about fishing." No one answered. Finally Peally said, "Our friends are waiting, Tommy. Are you going to help me or not?"

Tommy looked over his shoulder and shrugged. "We'll all be up later to help."

Tommy turned back and started reeling in the line, so he didn't see the hateful look Peally directed first at Collette and then at Roger.

Roger held up both hands and grinned.

"Hey, lady, don't waste any nasty looks on me. I don't even *like* volleyball!"

Collette laughed and waited till Peally had vanished into the pine trees at the top of the hill before she slowly stretched back her arm and then cast off in a long, graceful swing.

The line cut through the sunlight before it landed twenty feet from the dock, bobbing gently on the lake.

Roger and Tommy both clapped and whistled. Tommy patted Collette on the back. She grinned and pulled the hat down over her eyes so they couldn't see how really happy she was.

Chapter Thirteen

Collette wore her fishing hat for riding lessons later. She smiled all over again as she remembered the shocked and then excited looks on Sarah's and Marsha's faces as Collette told them all about the fishing lesson.

"I can't believe Roger stayed the whole time," Sarah laughed. "He sat between you and Tommy the whole time?"

"I can," snapped Marsha. "Roger has the sensitivity of a rock."

Collette stopped her horse and waited for Marsha to catch up. Marsha was afraid of horses and refused to ride one. But since she didn't want to be left out of anything, she insisted on walking hers on the trail while Sarah and Collette rode.

"What are you going to do about the diary?" asked Sarah. She looked as worried as Collette felt.

"I say let's go to Peally's cabin, ransack the place, and get the diary back before she can read another page of it," announced Marsha. She jerked her horse out from the bushes and yanked the reins to get him back on the trail.

"When should we plan this little raid, Marsha?" asked Collette. "Peally is always around. She would have us arrested if we were caught."

"Collette, we have to do something. Unless you didn't write anything worth keeping secret in that diary." Marsha snorted. "And we all know that isn't true. I never got to read a single page."

"We'll have to think of a plan when we get back to the cabin," said Collette. "Which will be *never* unless you hurry up, Marsha. You would be able to control that horse better from the saddle, you know."

Sarah laughed. Marsha had been leading the huge horse around for the past hour. The rest of the class had deserted them forty minutes ago.

"Go ahead and laugh," grunted Marsha as she tugged her horse ahead. "Any minute now your beast could have a crazed attack and charge right off a cliff. Then I will *walk* my horse back to camp and get help."

"Speaking of help," said Collette slowly. "I think I know when we can help ourselves to my diary in Peally's cabin."

"When?" Sarah asked.

"She mentioned a volleyball game they would have after dinner. She said it was only for her friends, so she wouldn't even get suspicious it we weren't there."

"Stop eating that grass, you dumb horse!" moaned Marsha. "What if they play volleyball outside her cabin?"

"I'll find out as much as I can," said Collette.

"I just hope we get there in time." Sarah bit her lip and started looking worried all over again. "Peally doesn't like you, Collette. I bet she'd love to tell the whole camp your most private secrets."

"Yeah," added Marsha. "All those private secrets you wouldn't even tell us."

Collette looked over at Sarah and was glad to see her smiling back. Sarah understood that keeping a diary secret wasn't the same thing as keeping a secret from a friend.

"I'll get it back, even if I have to walk right up to her and ask for it."

Collette let her horse trot on, enjoying its slow rocking and wishing she could relax enough to enjoy herself on such a beautiful day.

Peally would deny ever taking it, even if Collette found it in her trunk. Then she would get madder than ever.

Sneaking into someone's cabin to snoop was not a nice thing to do. Collette knew that. But neither was stealing, and that was exactly what Peally had done in the first place. She'd started off the whole rotten business by trying to act like she owned the camp and everyone in it.

"We'll go to Peally's cabin tonight during the volleyball game," Collette announced firmly. "Unless it rains."

Marsha squinted up at the clear blue sky. "Not a chance of rain. Don't look so worried, Collette. Snooping into other people's cabins is all part of camp life, like a ritual. Don't go thinking this thing to death like you usually do. Just relax, and we'll have your diary back by lights out."

Collette looked down at her watch. "We'd better hurry, or we'll miss dinner. Edith-Ann will send out a search party for sure."

Marsha nodded, strolling alongside her horse as if she were walking a large dog. "I'm starving. I never knew horseback riding was so much work."

Collette reached down and patted the chestnut coat of her own horse. Too bad Laura, Jeff, and Stevie couldn't see her now with her nice fishing hat and huge horse. She looked like a real camper.

By the time the girls had returned their horses and washed their hands, they were almost the last to stagger into the dining hall. Edith-Ann had left a short note in the cabin, saying she couldn't wait for them any longer and would see them after dinner.

As soon as they entered the main dining room they could hear the laughter. They smiled and looked around to see what was so funny.

Peally was standing on the tiny stage in the

front of the room holding a sheet of typing paper in her hand. She gripped the microphone, and she was shouting something out over the roar of laughter.

"Oh brother, look at that old show-off Peally," said Marsha. "What is she doing up there, reading a camp report or something?"

The girls each took a tray and hurried down the line. Marsha slammed a plate of potato salad down, saying "It's probably titled 'Ten Quick Ways To Become a Mean Person.' "

Collette rolled an apple across her tray, a slight frown beginning to set on her face. She turned slowly from the food to stare at Peally. Certain words were pelting against her like stones, bruising her with their familiarity.

" '. . . He looks cute wet or dry. He's Calvary Camp's cutest guy . . .' " Peally shouted in her clear, loud voice. Her eyes met Collette's. They were sparkling.

As the room exploded with more laughter, Collette began to search the room for Tommy. She saw him sitting with Roger and a table of other boys. They were all laughing, even Tommy.

"What is she reading to them?" asked Sarah with a giggle. "Probably one of those sappy romance books."

Collette stepped backward, knocking Sarah's tray to the floor. Her heart froze. She knew exactly what Peally was reading to the crowded dining room.

Her diary!

Chapter Fourteen

Peally held her hand up and waited for everyone to stop laughing. "Wait now, there's more, guys! All right . . . 'Dear Diary, I think he wants to kiss me . . .' "

The dining hall broke into hoots and foot-stamping.

Peally smiled out and waited a second before continuing.

" '. . . but he is too shy. Maybe he will get some more courage tomorrow. I hope so.' "

Peally held up the piece of paper and took a bow as everyone clapped.

"Collette . . . *Collette*, you are standing on my sandwich," Sarah said, nudging her gently. "What is wrong with you? You're as white as a ghost."

Collette took a step back, shivering and blinking as she stared straight at Peally. "She is making that part up. I never wrote anything about kissing. . . ."

"No . . ." said Sarah, reaching out and grabbing Collette's hand. "That's . . . that's your diary!"

Marsha spun around and glared at Peally. Then she turned back. "So how much did we miss?"

"Marsha!" Sarah yanked Marsha's arm.

"She's reading it to the whole camp!" Collette whispered hoarsely. She grabbed her tray, moving it down the food shelf as the apple rolled around.

"Now . . . listen, guys, listen!" Peally shouted from the stage. "You can hear another section from the mystery diary tomorrow night, so come early to get a good seat. Maybe I will announce the author of the diary and name her handsome prince. After all, we all know the handsome hunk is someone at Calvary Camp this week."

The dining hall broke into cheers and whistles. Peally took another bow and walked slowly away from the microphone Mr. Harrison always used for morning announcements.

Collette stopped, then willed herself to keep moving, knowing Peally would be watching her. She set down her tray on an empty table and walked toward the door.

"Hey, Collette!" called Sarah. "Where are you going?"

Collette caught up with Peally by the side exit. Peally saw her coming and actually waited for her. She slowly folded the paper in half and smiled. It was a mean smile. The kind the witch wore before she gave Snow White the poisoned apple.

"Give it back," Collette said.

Peally leaned back against the wall, crossing her arms and grinning. Things were going exactly the way she wanted them to.

"Give it back?" repeated Peally, raising her eyebrows. "Give it back, like I asked your friends to give me back my cabin? That kind of 'give it back'?"

Collette held out her hand, hoping Peally wouldn't notice how badly it was shaking. "Give me back my diary." How dare Peally use a part of Collette, reading it out loud for a side show!

"I bet you do miss your diary," Peally said

slowly. "My goodness, you wrote page after page every day, didn't you?"

Collette kept her hand out.

"How about a trade?" suggested Peally. She wasn't smiling anymore. She took a step closer to Collette as if she meant business and wanted to close the deal quickly.

"Trade? I never took anything from you," Collette shot back. If Peally meant the stupid cabin, let her take it. Let her shove the green dresser aside and stare at the red painted heart until she was blue in the face.

"The diary . . . for Tommy."

The words shot through Collette like bullets. Tommy?

Peally reached out and patted the fishing hat on Collette's head. "I wore that hat once, kiddo, so don't puff yourself up like some prized chicken. The only reason Tommy spends any time with you is that he's mad at me. Mad at me because I was hanging around with some kids at school that he didn't care for. . . ."

Peally stopped and stared at Collette with her nose turned up. As if Collette didn't count at all.

"That's the only reason he's wasting his time on a little rug rat like you." Peally shook her head at the very idea of it. "You're out of your league, Murphy. You know it, I know it, and tomorrow after I read another diary selection, Tommy will know it."

The room seemed too warm, too loud, all of a sudden. Collette leaned her head against the wall, determined not to faint in front of someone as awful as Peally.

Peally laughed. "Seems like there isn't too much of a choice anymore, is there, Collette?"

Sarah and Marsha came up, each putting a hand on Collette's arm.

"Are you okay?" Marsha asked. She shoved in between Peally and Collette. "Just ignore everything Peally says."

Peally laughed. "She's fine. She'll feel a whole lot better when she makes a few smart decisions. Right, Collette?"

Peally handed Collette the folded paper. "Here, read this over again. It might help you decide faster. Only the names have been omitted to protect the guilty. And remember, Collette. I can make up any diary pages I want, to make it more interesting."

Collette kept her hands by her side. She looked over at Peally, then shoved her hands in her pockets.

"No."

It was quiet for a minute before Peally shrugged and crumpled up the paper, letting it drop to the floor.

"Fine with me. I have the original, after all."

Collette kicked at the balled-up paper, sending it closer to Peally. "I mean no . . . no to your trade."

Peally's eyes got wide. She looked more shocked than mad.

"You have no idea how rough things can get for you at camp, Collette. You've never played hardball with me before."

Without being sure her knees would move, Collette brushed past Peally and walked away.

"You'll be the laughingstock of this camp by tomorrow night, Murphy. I promise you that!"

Collette kept walking. Part of her wanted to go to Edith-Ann and tell her everything, sure that Edith-Ann would welcome the opportunity to solve a huge problem and feel like a needed counselor.

But the other part of her wanted to find a way out of this herself. Peally had to be conquered by an equal, so she would finally stop acting like the queen of Calvary Camp.

Collette took a deep breath and winced. Part of her was so scared, it hurt!

Chapter Fifteen

"Collette, are you *sure* you saw Peally at the volleyball game?" Sarah wrung her hands together for the twelfth time. "We have to be absolutely positive she won't be anywhere near her cabin or we'll be caught!"

"Yes, I saw her. She was hanging all over Tommy like some sort of moss."

"But Tommy shook her off every time, Collette," reminded Marsha.

Collette shrugged. She was getting so mixed up. What if Peally was telling the truth, and Tommy really liked Peally? What if he was just being nice to Collette to make Peally jealous and teach her a lesson?

"I think this is their cabin." Marsha looked down at her scrap of paper. "Yeah, Amber wrote it down for me. Cabin eleven. Peally sleeps closest to the door, bottom bunk."

"I hope Amber won't tell anyone," Sarah said. "We could get kicked out of camp for this."

Collette pushed through the white pines and walked to the back of the cabin. All three girls crouched under the large window in the back. "Amber won't tell. She's nice."

Slowly Collette stood up, looking through the screen into the cabin. It was empty, filled only with the shadows of early evening.

Marsha reached out and jiggled the screen, smiling as it broke free and fell into her hands.

"Amber was great to sneak in here and unlock this for us."

Sarah helped Marsha set the screen gently against a tree. "No one would think anything about Amber walking into Peally's cabin. She's friendly with everyone at camp."

Collette took a deep breath and then swung her leg over the low window sill. Pulling herself up, she rolled across her tummy and into the cabin.

Then she turned around and helped pull Marsha and Sarah into the room.

Marsha began to stride up and down the cabin, picking up robes and tennis shoes.

"There's not one classy bit of clothing in this entire cabin. Who would wear something this tacky, even to camp?"

Sarah pushed back the curtains of the closet, looking behind hangers and running her hand across the narrow top shelf.

Collette walked straight to the small dresser near Peally's bed. She picked up a small silver picture frame. A smiling Tommy looked out at her.

"Take Tommy's picture out and keep it till the last day of camp, Collette," whispered Marsha. "She owes you."

Collette quickly put it back, feeling guilty enough for snooping. "No. He probably gave it to her . . . last year, maybe."

As Collette bent to look under Peally's bed, she glanced back up at the picture. Maybe he did give it to her this year. They both lived in town. Maybe they really did like each other.

"Find anything?" asked Sarah. She looked under a pillow, then carefully put it back in place.

"No."

"What in the world is going on?" hissed Marsha. She stomped over and tossed Peally's pillow across the room. "We aren't maid service, girls. This is supposed to be a ransacking expedition." Marsha ripped the sheets off Peally's bed, dumping them in a pile near the door. "Now get busy."

Collette and Sarah exchanged smiles. They watched as Marsha unscrewed toothpaste caps and squirted the white paste up and down the center of the cabin.

Collette opened Peally's trunk, riffling through T-shirts and shorts on the floor, searching. Her diary wasn't anywhere.

"We'll teach them a thing or two about messing with the Sacred Heart girls," Marsha mumbled.

Collette continued to search, opening drawers, looking under mattresses. She didn't want to mess up the cabin. She just wanted her diary, that was all. She just wanted what was hers.

"Let's not break anything," she warned.

"Girls!" shrieked Edith-Ann.

The girls looked up, their mouths frozen in three identical O's.

"Peally is on her way up here with half the camp, including the director, Mr. Harrison. How did she know you were here . . . doing this? Let's get out, now."

Edith-Ann closed the wooden door, and pointed to the window. Marsha flew out, followed by Collette and Sarah. The three turned and watched as Edith-Ann made an impressive leap out the window.

"Run for the west section of the lake by the fishing hut, and don't stop till you get there. I'll catch up and insist we've all been there swimming for hours."

Collette and Sarah grabbed hands and shot through the dark woods. Marsha was already yards ahead, her thin, scared wail trailing her like smoke.

"Why is Edith-Ann helping us out of this mess?" Collette panted, as they slid down the moss-covered hillside. "I thought she'd turn us in for sure."

Sarah shook her head, too winded to speak.

Collette slowed, seeing the glimmering reflection of the water ahead. Edith-Ann took her job very seriously. She probably didn't want it to go on her record that her entire cabin had turned into snoopers and ransackers.

The next day Edith-Ann would probably have them scrub the entire floor of the cabin with toothbrushes as punishment for bringing shame to cabin seven.

In the dusk, Collette shivered once, then shivered again. Tomorrow would be even worse.

Tomorrow Peally would read sections of her diary at breakfast, lunch, and dinner. By the time Games Day was over, Collette would not be able to look anyone in the face again, especially Tommy.

"I'm here," puffed Edith-Ann. She picked herself up from the bottom of the hillside and tried to adjust her fogged-up glasses.

The three girls stood at attention, ready to hear the worst of it first. Edith-Ann looked upset. She was already twisting her whistle around and around in her hands, probably imagining she had their skinny little necks in her grips.

"What you girls did was. . . ."

Edith-Ann pulled down her glasses, rubbing her hands over her eyes before shoving the glasses back up the bridge of her nose.

". . . perfectly understandable under the circumstances," she finished.

"What?" Marsha broke into a wide smile and grabbed Edith-Ann by the arm. "You're not mad?"

Edith-Ann began to smile, shaking her head.

"I heard about the diary from one of the other counselors. I figured it was yours, Collette. Reading someone's else's diary out loud should be a felony."

Collette smiled back. She hadn't realized Edith-Ann had known about her diary.

"Then I checked underneath the green dresser. When I saw it was gone, I decided to try and find you girls before it was too late."

Sarah threw her hands up in the air and started to dance in a happy circle by the lake. "Thank you, oh, thank you, Edith-Ann. You are the world's greatest counselor!"

Collette sighed. "But we still don't have the diary." She was glad that Edith-Ann was on their side, but that just meant that now four people were looking for the missing diary instead of three.

Edith-Ann held up both hands like a sheriff.

"Leave it to me, girls. I'll work out a plan. Go jump in the lake and get wet before someone comes up. If our alibi is going to be swimming, we need wet swimmers."

Marsha and Sarah started to laugh as they stepped out of their shorts and pulled their sweatshirts over their heads.

Edith-Ann leaned against the tree and consulted her clipboard. "Now, we have to work fast if we want to prevent chapter two of your life from being read over breakfast."

Collette tried to smile, but her mouth wiggled too much. She felt like crying. Maybe she should have struck some sort of agreement with Peally. But she couldn't trade Tommy around like he was a prize. She couldn't give him back. He belonged to himself.

Edith-Ann gave her back a few comforting pats.

"Just tell me that things are going to be all right," whispered Collette.

"It will be all right," Edith-Ann announced firmly.

As the two of them watched Marsha doing handstands and Sarah diving backward in the shadowy water, Collette repeated to herself. "It will be all right. It will be all right."

With a deep sigh, she lowered her head to her knees. She was too tired to believe anything else.

Chapter Sixteen

Thursday morning, Collette's eyes were open before the birds came out in full force. Edith-Ann had not been able to think of a way to get the diary back. Nothing short of going to Mr. Harrison and telling him the whole mixed-up story was going to do any good. Even that wouldn't guarentee anything. They didn't have any proof. Just a whole heart full of hurt.

Collette closed her eyes and felt a hot, fat tear roll down the curve of her nose.

"Noooooooooooooooooo!!!!"

Collette's head flew off the pillow. Marsha stood in the center of her bed, with both hands covering her face. She screamed again.

"Noooooooooooooooo!!!"

In a flash, Edith-Ann and Sarah flew out of their beds and ran over to Marsha.

Collette flipped back her sheet and hurried to Marsha's bed. She couldn't believe it. Marsha's face was red and puffy. Both eyes were narrowed to slits.

"Look at me!"

Edith-Ann ran to the dresser and grabbed her glasses. Shoving them up on her nose, she walked around the bed, studying Marsha. "Looks like poison to me!"

"Poison!" Marsha dropped to her knees and cried even harder. "It was that dumb potato salad!"

Edith-Ann patted Marsha's back. "No, I meant poison ivy or oak."

Collette looked at Sarah, reaching out a hand. Poor Marsha! Quickly Collette snatched back her hand.

"Sarah!" cried Collette. "Look at *your* face!"

Sarah yelled before she could even look, then screamed again as she ran and stood in front of the mirror.

Marsha hopped off her bed and ran to look at Sarah's face. They both cried and screamed some more.

"Calm down girls," called out Edith-Ann. "Let's have a look."

"We must have put my sweatshirt in the poison ivy," cried Marsha. "Remember, we both dried off our faces with it?"

Sarah and Marsha hugged each other and cried their hardest. Collette walked over to them both, but patted them on the shoulders instead of giving them a real hug.

"My face feels like it's on fire!" Sarah sobbed.

"My face feels like it's about to explode," wailed Marsha. "Look at my beautiful eyes. They're ruined forever!"

Edith-Ann yanked on her robe and then bent under the bed and pulled out a huge book.

"I'm sure poison ivy is in here. Every ailment that can occur at camp is in here!"

"I hope it isn't poison oak," Sarah wailed. "My cousin Larry had it once, and it took ten days before his own mother wanted to kiss him good night."

With that Sarah began to cry even harder. "Look at me! I have it on my face, on my legs!"

Marsha walked with both arms outstretched like a zombie. "I am covered with it. All of our clothes must have been on top of a whole patch of it."

Edith-Ann closed her book with a quick thump and tossed it onto her bed. "Get dressed, girls. I'm not sure what you have, but you definitely have something. I'll have to take you to the infirmary before it spreads over every square inch of your bodies!"

Marsha lifted her head and wailed like a coyote.

Sarah plucked at her sweatshirt. "I want to go home. I want my own doctor to look at this. Not some camp doctor who doesn't even know me."

Marsha yanked her nightgown off and scowled at her stomach. "I'm going home. I've had it with this camp!"

"Let's *all* go home," sniffed Sarah. "We can have our own banquet at my house. Pizza and pink lotion for our poison!"

Collette sat down on her bed. Poor Sarah and Marsha! They would miss Games Day today and the banquet on Friday . . . the nicest parts of camp.

"My mom will drive up and get us, girls. We have the biggest car, and it's air-conditioned. At least the cold will freeze our itching."

Edith-Ann buttoned her shorts and stepped into her tennis shoes and walked out the door. "Hurry and get dressed, girls. Collette, maybe you can start packing while we're gone."

"Collette, don't forget our tennis rackets, okay?" reminded Sarah. "And my camera is on the top shelf of the closet."

"And your tennis racket is next to my bed, Collette," Marsha said. She yanked on a T-shirt and winced as she pulled shorts over her red, rashy legs. "Don't forget to leave a note for Tommy. Kind of a good-bye sort of thing."

Edith-Ann checked her watch. "Might as well pull the sheets off everyones' beds, Collette."

Collette stood up. "Well, I'm glad to help pack for Sarah and Marsha, but . . . well, I don't have poison ivy, so why am I going home?"

Everyone stopped in mid-step and stared at Collette.

"I mean . . ." Collette closed her mouth. She wasn't exactly sure what she meant, but she didn't want to go home. Nothing was settled about camp. She didn't have her diary back, she didn't have a chance to say a proper good-bye to Tommy Hansley. . . .

"You can't stay here by yourself!" insisted Marsha. "Peally would eat you alive without Sarah and me here to protect you!"

"Collette, what fun could you have all by yourself?" Sarah asked.

"I thought it might be fun to stay for Games Day," Collette began. "Win a trophy for cabin seven."

Marsha touched her face gently and started to cry. "How can you even think about a dumb trophy, when Sarah and I might end up in the hospital with poisoning of the face!"

Marsha slammed her trunk shut.

"Collette is right," said Edith-Ann. "There's no reason why she should leave."

Sarah sat on the edge of Collette's bed. "But don't you *want* to go home, Collette?"

Sarah's eyes were red-rimmed. Collette couldn't tell if she were about to cry or if her rash was just getting worse.

"She won't miss us a bit, Sarah," blurted out Marsha. "She would rather stay here and talk to Tommy Hansley than come home and be our friend."

"She is our friend," Sarah said quickly. "Oh, come on. Let's get down to the nurse. My back feels like it has blisters!"

"You girls are going to be so busy with ointment and resting, you wouldn't have time to visit with Collette, anyway," Edith-Ann announced.

"I feel so awful," sniffed Marsha. She picked up her brush and tried to run it through her hair. "Ohhhh, I can't even brush my hair. I have poisoned hair!"

Sarah handed Collette a handful of stamps and envelopes.

"I want a letter tonight and tomorrow. Tell me everything, since . . . well, you know, since the diary is gone."

"Me, too!" cried Marsha. She pulled open her trunk and handed Collette a pale blue stationery box. "This is really expensive paper, but I don't care how much you use. Use as much as it takes to tell me every single thing that happens while I'm gone."

Collette laughed. She reached out and tried to give both girls a hug, but all three froze at the same minute and broke apart, laughing.

Collette watched from the window as Edith-Ann led the way down the path.

"You would think this camp would get rid of all that poison ivy before they allowed kids to come up here," Marsha grumbled loudly, waving her arms at the surrounding forest. "My dad will be furious!"

Sitting down on top of Marsha's trunk, Collette stared at her own. Maybe she should surprise Marsha and Sarah and have hers packed, too.

Tommy never *did* come right out and say he wanted to sit with Collette at the banquet Friday. Besides, Peally was bound to read more awful parts of the diary today at breakfast and lunch.

By dinner, Peally would announce to the whole camp that the author of camp's sappiest romance novel was Collette Murphy. Then Tommy would be so embarrassed to be part of such a story he would stay as far away from Collette as he could.

"Phooey," whispered Collette, looking outside at the sun filtering through the trees. If only she knew what today was going to bring. Should she play it safe and go home or take a chance and stay?

Collette glanced at the white fishing hat hanging from her bed post and smiled.

Outside, the morning breakfast bell was ringing. Games Day had begun!

Chapter Seventeen

Collette continued waving until Mrs. Cessano's pale-blue BMW was out of sight. It was already afternoon.

"Sarah and Marsha will be fine," Edith-Ann assured her. She gave Collette's ponytail a tug. "We'd better hurry and get down to the dock. They are going to start choosing teams for the relays any minute." Edith-Ann handed Collette a sandwich wrapped in a napkin. "Here, eat this on the way. I knew you would be busy saying good-bye, so I stopped in the cafeteria to get you some lunch."

"Was . . ." Collette took a small bite of the sandwich. Should she ask Edith-Ann if Peally had been on stage reading another page of her diary? Or was it better just to pretend it wasn't happening?

"Peally read another page, but there was nothing that gave it away as being your diary," Edith-Ann said gently.

"What . . . what did I say?"

"Something about a present at the marshmallow roast, and how you want to give him the nickname, Mr. Muscle."

Before Edith-Ann could even finish, Collette's face turned beet red. Peally was so mean. By tonight she would start naming names.

"It would be great if you could take home a blue ribbon to the girls." Edith-Ann smiled at Collette. "You know, Collette, with a name like Edith-Ann, a person runs into a lot of Peallys in life. I sure gave them a lot of material. Thick glasses, bookworm, overweight. . . ."

Collette looked up and felt a little embarassed. Edith-Ann was reading her mental diary to Collette. Offering a page to help Collette feel better.

"The funny part is . . ." Edith-Ann stopped and thought. "The funny part is, both of us are targets for the Peallys but for opposite reasons. I was kind of a . . . a nerd, I guess. And you are a target because you're pretty and nice."

"You're not a nerd!" insisted Collette quickly. Her face flashed red again as she thought of all the times she'd giggled when Edith-Ann had marched into the room with a clipboard and whistle attached.

Edith-Ann laughed and waved Collette out the door.

"Hey, I wouldn't be going to college to study how to teach kids if I held any grudges. Come on. Let's get down there and show Calvary Camp what cabin seven is all about. If you win today, they will give you a trophy at their banquet on Friday."

Collette grabbed Tommy's fishing cap and stuck it on her head.

"Looks great, kiddo!"

Collette smiled back at Edith-Ann, with her baggy shorts and rolled-down socks.

"Edith-Ann, do . . . would you mind if I wore your whistle today? Sort of a good-luck piece?"

Edith-Ann's face flushed pink as she took off her whistle and held it out to Collette. "Just give a whistle if you need me."

Collette heard the loud shouts and laughter before she reached the top of the path leading down to the lake. She looked over and smiled at Edith-Ann. Games Day was going to be fun. All the kids sounded like they were in a really good party mood.

"I see Roger and Tommy," said Collette. "They're both wearing orange sashes."

"Must be captains of the orange team." Edith-Ann squinted. "Peally and Lorraine are captains of the blue team."

Collette laughed. "I don't think Peally is going to pick me."

Edith-Ann reached out and pulled Collette back with her hand. "Collette, I don't want to worry you, but. . . ."

Collette's heart contracted just a bit. "But what?"

"Peally was blabbing to everyone who would listen that you and Marsha and Sarah were the ones who broke into her cabin and messed things up. I just thought you should know. She kept saying that you broke her picture frame and a lot of other stuff."

"We didn't break anything!"

"Of course not. I was there. I'm sure no one believed her anyway. I blew my whistle and told the whole group that you and the girls were with me, swimming. That's how they got the poison ivy."

Collette nodded, knowing that Peally could argue that Collette Murphy didn't have a speck of poison ivy. Maybe she was back breaking things instead of swimming.

Even with the hot afternoon sun beating down, Collette felt a sudden chill. Each day she was surprised all over again that Peally would spend so much time trying to make Collette's life miserable.

"Collette!"

Amber ran up from the dock, waving her arm. Her orange scarf was tied around her neck, cowgirl-style.

"Boy, am I glad to see you. I was afraid that you would go home with Sarah and Marsha. Too bad about the poison ivy."

Edith-Ann gave Collette a quick pat on the shoulder and went off to talk to Fred.

Collette let Amber lead her down to the kids still waiting to be picked for the two teams. Collette stood right in front of Tommy. She ducked her head so she wouldn't laugh right out loud with happiness.

"Annie, Allison . . . Devin," called out Tommy.

Collette looked up and grinned at Tommy. Of course he couldn't call out her name the moment she walked up.

"Carmen, Courtney . . ." Peally paused and chewed on her little finger. "Let me see. This is getting hard with only six left."

Peally tapped her long fingernails against her cheek.

"How about . . . eenie, meenie, minee, moe . . . Jamie."

Tommy looked over at Peally and grinned. "Good idea, Peally. Eenie, meenie, minee, moe . . . Liza, Nathan, and . . ."

Collette let a giggle slip out. She looked up at Tommy and raised an eyebrow and gave him the big smile she couldn't hide any longer. He was such a big tease. Any minute now he would scratch his head, give his slow, lopsided grin, and say, Collette Murphy!

"Ryan," Tommy finished quietly.

Collette's smile slid off her face.

Peally reached over and gave Tommy's arm a little squeeze, giggling so hard she had to wait a minute before she could talk again.

"Okay . . . okay. Now there are three campers left. I get to pick first, then Tommy and . . . oh, boo-hoo, there will be one left over."

Peally gave a fake pout, as if it was just breaking her heart that someone would be standing there, red-faced and unpicked.

Collette looked to her left and right. Petey Greenberg, a skinny little eight-year-old who was allergic to grass, and ten-year-old Marty Watts, who only came to Calvary Camp because his over-eaters' camp had a long waiting list.

Roger was staring at Collette, so she gave him a smile. Roger knew Collette wasn't good in gym class, but he must know that Tommy and Collette had been spending a lot of time together lately. He wouldn't be surprised or mad when Tommy chose her next. Maybe Tommy didn't choose her right away because it would have been too obvious, too unfair to the others.

Collette tried not to smile too broadly. Actually she wished that Tommy would choose her and the remaining camper too, so nobody would have to feel left out.

She'd whisper it to Tommy just as soon as he picked her.

"You go first, Tommy," insisted Peally in her fake voice. "I just can't make a decision. The choices here are so interesting."

Everyone snickered, and a few campers started to whisper behind covered hands.

Tommy just stood there, looking at the three of them like it was the biggest decision of his life.

Roger finally leaned over and whispered something, but Tommy just shook his head, annoyed at whatever Roger had suggested.

Collette couldn't help but glare at Roger. Surely he hadn't tried to talk Tommy out of picking her, just because she didn't make A's in gym class.

"Eenie, meenie . . ." Tommy took a step closer. "Murphy . . ."

Just as Collette broke into a smile and took a step closer, Tommy finished with a loud "NO!"

"Eenie, meenie, Murphy, no," repeated Peally. "That has a real cute ring to it."

The wave of laughter that followed hit Collette like a metal sheet.

"Collette Murphy," called out Roger. He reached across Tommy's arm and pulled Collette into line next to him.

The campers grew quiet; the whispering stopped.

"Tommy is the real captain, Roger," Peally said. "He is in charge of picking the teams."

"Yeah, well I'm co-captain, sweetheart," Roger shot back. "Petey, you're blue, and Marty, we need you with us."

Mr. Harrison gave three quick toots on his whistle and marched over to the groups.

"Are we ready, blue and orange?" he shouted out in a happy voice. "Remember, the first leg of the race is to canoe out to the island. Once there, grab your color flag and get back to the dock as soon as possible. Break into groups of three, and get to your canoes!"

No one moved. Everyone was watching Peally and Tommy whisper to each other.

Mr. Harrison gave a long, shrill toot on his whistle.

"What is the problem?"

Mr. Harrison waited a minute before he started giving little pushes toward the canoes.

Other counselors started pushing shoulders, too, and pretty soon most of the canoes were heading out toward Mouse Island.

"Come on, Tom," called Roger as he headed for the canoe. "We're wasting time."

Mr. Harrison put his large hand on Collette's head. "Tommy always seems to pick the cutest girl for his team," he added with a hearty laugh.

Collette watched Tommy's face, looking for a smile. But Tommy and Peally only exchanged a quick look before they each turned and headed toward the canoes.

"Come on, Collette," called Roger. He sped past

her and handed her an orange scarf.

Tommy and Roger each had an oar in hand by the time Collette reached the canoe. She wasn't even seated before they dug into the shallow bottom and shoved off.

The thrust of the tiny canoe shot Collette backward, hitting the small of her back against the seat.

Tommy was right behind her, but he didn't even try to help her up.

Collette turned and searched for a clue in Tommy's angry face. What had she done to make him mad? Did Roger really tell how poorly she did in gym class?

"Sorry . . . I guess you wanted someone a little more athletic on your team," said Collette. She waited for him to say something back, like, "Oh, no, you'll be fine," or "We'll make a good team, Collette."

But Tommy never even looked at her; instead he stared straight ahead as he quickly dipped the oar in and out of the water, as if a killer shark were chasing them across the lake.

"Too bad about Marsha and Sarah," Roger shouted as he half turned in his seat. "You sure were lucky not to get it."

Collette nodded, all set to tell them what the nurse had said about the poison ivy, when Tommy broke in.

"Serves them right for tramping through the woods at night, sneaking into people's cabins, break — " Collette spun around so fast the canoe tipped sharply to the right.

How did Tommy know about them going into Peally's cabin? Did Edith-Ann have to fill out a report after all? Did Marsha let something slip at the infirmary?

"They . . . we were all swimming in the lake," began Collette quickly. "I think they dropped their clothes in a patch of poison ivy. . . ."

Tommy gave a hard, loud laugh. But it wasn't the kind of laugh you gave over something funny. It was the kind that made you feel like you were the joke.

"And we all know why you didn't get any poison ivy, right, Collette? Because we all know that you decided not to go swimming."

"Right . . ." Collette slowly turned around, her cheeks blazing. How did Tommy know she was the only one not swimming? Was he hiding in the bushes the whole time? Would he have done that? Was he in the bushes while poor Marsha and Sarah were in their underwear?

"No swimming for Collette," continued Tommy in a tight voice. "She had other things to do last night."

Tommy lifted his paddle and slapped it down so hard it sprayed the back of Collette's shirt.

"More important things than swimming, Roger."

With her eyes locked on the island ahead, Collette tried to sort things out. For some reason Tommy was upset because she didn't go swimming.

Collette felt her heart sinking inch by inch. She swatted at a group of gnats swirling in front of her. Something was wrong, and it was more than the swimming.

"Tommy, why don't you just shut up and concentrate on getting to the island?" Roger shouted from the front.

Tommy laughed again, dropping his oar to the floor of the canoe. "Hey, Mr. Bodyguard, why don't you just do all the rowing? It was your idea to include Collette on our team. I sure didn't want her."

"That's right," snapped Roger. "And she'll be more help than you are!"

Tommy laughed. "You guys really stick together, don't you? Maybe you were with Collette last night at my cabin. Maybe that's how she got away with it."

Collette spun around and grabbed the fishing hat off her head, throwing it down next to Tommy.

"What are you talking about? What did I get away with?"

Tommy took the hat and looked at it for a minute before he tossed it out into the lake. Then he looked straight into Collette's eyes.

"Breaking the best fishing rod I've ever owned."

Chapter Eighteen

"I *WHAT*?"

Collette made such a huge gasp, she sucked in a gnat or two. "I never broke your fishing rod," she sputtered. She wiped her hand across her mouth and leaned closer to Tommy. "Who told you I broke your fishing rod?"

Tommy completely ignored her question, leaning sideways to catch Roger's attention.

"Hey Rog, do you know how many cans of tuna I had to shelve to buy that rod? Can you even imagine how many Saturdays I spent breaking my back, bagging groceries, unpacking crate after crate — "

Tommy broke off, as if he couldn't even stand to talk about it anymore.

"I didn't do it!" Collette cried.

"I know you did, Collette."

Roger lifted his oar, and the canoe slowed. "At least give her a chance to explain, Tommy. I mean, the whole idea of Collette Murphy doing something illegal is stupid. She never even has an overdue library book, for Pete's sake. She isn't the type to break — "

Tommy raised his arm and swatted away Roger's words.

"You two are old buddies, so you stick together. I'm the one who worked hard for that fishing rod, so I — "

"Yeah," Roger gave his oar a kick. "So big deal, and aren't we all proud of you. Think you're the only kid in America who ever worked after school?"

"Oh, stop it," cried Collette. "Stop yelling about everything. Just tell me how I got tied up with this fishing rod mystery. When did someone break it?"

Tommy rolled his eyes and gave a mean smile.

"At least tell her what she's accused of, Tommy."

The lake was quiet. Finally, Tommy gave out a deep sigh, picked up his oar, and started moving the canoe closer to the island.

"Forget it," he said hoarsely.

"Peally came up to Tommy last night and told him that you broke into her cabin and smashed the picture frame with his picture in it. Then they went inside his cabin and found the broken fishing rod."

"So . . . so what makes Peally the boss? How does she know I did any of that?"

Tommy tapped Collette on the shoulder. "Peally had proof, Collette. I didn't want to believe her at first. I didn't believe her till this morning."

Collette bit the inside of her lip so she wouldn't show how near tears she was.

"I've known Peally since she was five. I guess it's safe to believe her."

Collette blinked hard. Why wasn't it safe to believe Collette Murphy? Was she so untrustworthy after only a few days?

Something inside Collette began to ache. Probably her soul or another secret part of her that had never been so bruised before.

On either side, canoes glided past on their return trip from the island, the captured flags snapping in the breeze.

Collette studied the sunlight as it seemed to float on the water. Too bad her dad wasn't in a nearby canoe. He was a lawyer, used to defending clients against huge corporations. He would know lots of things to say to regain trust and uncover lies.

Collette shivered with the ripples as the breeze blew past. Maybe her dad wouldn't know what to say, either. Maybe he would be just as confused. Maybe he had never come up against Peally. Maybe he'd never had to defend anyone against pure hate before.

As soon as the canoe neared the island, Tommy splashed out into the shallow water. He dragged the canoe a few feet up the rocky shore and then raced up the hill like someone escaping from a burning car.

"Don't worry about Tommy, Collette. He's just mad." Roger held out his hand, and Collette hopped to the shore. "I told him Peally was lying.

Boy, does that girl have it in for you."

Collette could feel the tears rimming her eyes.

"How come girls don't fight over me?" Roger asked. He jabbed Collette in the side and smiled. "How come?"

Collette laughed, then took a deep breath.

"Why is Peally's . . . word better than mine?"

Roger shrugged. "I don't know. Peally keeps calling you and me spoiled rich kids."

Collette started walking, her throat too full to speak. Tommy believed Peally, thinking she had more honor since she had less money.

"I didn't break the fishing rod, Roger. I didn't — " Collette clamped her mouth down on the rest of the words. They sounded weak, because they had been said so many times before.

"I got the flag; get back in the boat!" Tommy shouted from the top of the hill. "Two teams are still looking for their flags. At least we can beat them back."

Collette turned and walked back to the canoe. She waded into the lake, anxious to get back herself. She couldn't wait to pack her suitcases, call her mom, and get out of this mean camp.

Her mother wouldn't mind a bit if she left early. In fact, she would be thrilled to have Collette back with them. Her mom had written two letters already, and both her brothers and Laura had scribbled messages.

Even if her mom had to pack all the kids in the car and drive through rush-hour traffic, she would . . . smiling and happy and knowing her daughter would never break. . . .

Her tears stung, and Collette tried not to think of how much her mom loved her. It seemed too out of place, when she was surrounded by so many people who didn't even *like* her.

"Hey . . . Whoa . . . YAAAAAAAAAAA!"

"Tommy, Tommy!" Roger screamed.

Collette turned, her own hands flying out as she watched Tommy flip through the air like a rag doll, crashing down hard against the rocks.

Roger reached him first. He pulled Tommy to a sitting position, while brushing away the pine needles and dust.

"Hey, man, you really flew down that hill. Are you all right?"

Tommy gave a short nod, his face grimacing with pain. His left eye had a cut above it, and his arms were raked with clawlike scratches from the rocks.

"I hurt my leg. I really hurt my leg bad. . . ."

By the time Collette reached Tommy, his sock was already soaked clean through with blood. The cut was deep.

"You need stitches," Collette announced.

"No kidding." Tommy tried to get his leg away from Collette's hand but winced instead. "Hey . . . boy, this really hurts."

Roger looked back down at the cut, rubbing his hand back and forth across his head.

"Okay . . . okay," stammered Roger. "Now, we have to think of a plan. I mean, we are talking major bleeding here."

Collette reached up and tugged on Roger's T-shirt.

"Give me your shirt, Rog. Hurry."

"My shirt?" Roger looked confused and a little unhappy. "My new, never-even-been-worn-before shirt?"

Collette untied Tommy's laces and carefully

pulled off his shoe. She knew it hurt, but there wasn't a choice.

"Come on, Roger. I need something clean."

Roger took another peek at the blood, shuddering as he yanked the shirt off over his head.

After a quick shake, Collette folded it neatly into a thick rectangle. She wrapped it carefully around Tommy's ankle, then leaned into it with both palms.

Tommy grabbed his forehead with his hand, his shoulders sagging back against the rocks.

"Where did you learn that?" asked Roger. Collette couldn't tell if he was impressed or worried that she might be making things worse.

Collette shook off the question, not really interested in talking. She'd learned it last summer from her mom. Little Stevie had run in front of a metal swing and cracked his head open. Things looked pretty bad until her mom started running across the playground. As she passed Jeff she pulled off his shirt, rolling it as she ran to Stevie.

Her mother had applied direct pressure, wiped away Stevie's tears, and herded everyone into the car before the swing had even stopped moving.

But Collette wasn't going to talk about it now. Tommy would hold up his hand to interrupt her, announcing that he was sick of all the dull Murphy stories she'd been sharing during the past few days.

Collette stood and pulled a thin, tan belt from her green shorts. She wrapped the belt around the bandage, then looked up at Roger. "I need a knife or something sharp to poke another hole in the belt."

"I have one," said Tommy, pointing to his backpack near the rocks. His eyes locked briefly with Collette's before he looked away.

Tommy looked miserable. Collette picked up his backpack, trying not to think about it too much. His ankle was killing him, that was all.

Unzipping the backpack, Collette stuck her hand in. The sooner they got back to the camp, the sooner she could call her mom.

Collette pulled out a camera, a thick blue sweatshirt, a pack of crackers, and —

Her hand stopped.

Her diary!

Chapter Nineteen

"My diary," announced Collette in a hollow voice. She looked at Roger, who looked away, embarrassed. He must have known all along that Tommy had the diary.

"Where did you get this?" Collette was surprised her voice sounded so strong. Inside she felt like rubber.

"Peally," reported Roger. "She gave it to Tommy this morning."

Tommy suddenly came to life. He leaned closer, his face red with anger.

"Peally is my friend. She thought I should know what you've been writing in your diary."

Collette bent her head, her face scalding.

Tommy had read her diary! Read all those private, personal thoughts that she'd even kept from Sarah. . . . Pages about how green his eyes looked in the afternoon sun, how his strong, tanned arms gripped a baseball bat, how funny he was when he tried to teach her how to bait a hook.

Collette tried to swallow, tried to breathe. She felt like she was under a giant magnifying glass, surrounded by people who got to see every secret part of her, whether she liked it or not.

And what made it even sadder was that, after Tommy had read her most private thoughts and dreams, he no longer liked her.

"Yoo-hoo, found you!"

All three looked up, startled. Peally raced down the hill, waving her blue flag up and down like a tiny wing.

"I can't find Linda or Janet anywhere," Peally laughed. She shook back her long blonde hair and grinned at Tommy.

As soon as she noticed his foot, she dropped her flag and hurried over to his side.

"Oh, Tommy, poor Tommy, what happened to you?"

"Fell down the hill." Tommy tried to give her a carefree smile, as though it wasn't a big deal at all.

"Collette stopped the bleeding and bandaged his foot," Roger informed her. "Probably saved his life, in case you're interested, Peally."

Roger took a step closer to Collette, the four of them pairing off like they were about to start a dance instead of a fight.

Peally looked up and smiled, all the while patting Tommy's shoulder with her hand. "Well, Miss Florence Nightingale, thank you for helping Tommy."

Collette held tight to the diary, squeezing it so her hands wouldn't shake.

"Peally, why did you lie and tell Tommy that I broke his fishing rod?"

Peally didn't look a bit upset. She almost smiled.

"Actually, Collette, I didn't say a word. Your diary said it all."

Peally looked at the diary. She seemed almost happy that Collette knew Tommy had seen it.

"What?" Collette looked down at the diary.

"She's right, Collette," added Tommy. "Next

time you sneak in and break something, don't be dumb enough to record it."

Collette's eyes widened. Record it? Record *what*?

Boy, she had been dumb, all right. Dumb to write down every nice thing Tommy had ever said to her. She had recorded it so she could read and reread it again and again. Because it had once been so special.

She would never want to record today, not ever!

Collette sighed, lowering her arm.

Peally stood up and grabbed the diary from Collette.

"Allow me. . . ." Peally stood up straighter and started to read aloud. She started speaking before she had even searched for a page.

" 'Dear Diary, You will never guess what I just did. I snuck into Peally's cabin first, since I hate her guts, and then I went into Tommy's cabin and broke his favorite fishing rod. HA! HA! I don't even care. He spends too much time with that fishing rod. Fishing is so boring. Maybe now he will have free time and will ask me to the banquet. . . .' "

"I never wrote that!" cried Collette.

Roger stuck his chin over Peally's shoulder.

"That doesn't even look like her writing . . . too sloppy for Collette. Hey, this is a set-up, man!"

Peally laughed long and loud, as if Roger had just told a funny story.

"Of course it doesn't look like her writing, Roger. She was in such a hurry when she wrote it. She had such a busy, busy night. Everyone else was at the volleyball game, except Collette and her two awful friends."

"You told us we weren't invited, Peally," snapped Collette. "Remember?"

Without even answering, Peally tossed the diary down in the dirt by Collette's feet and walked back to Tommy.

"Come on, Tommy," she gushed. "Let Peally take you back to camp so the nurse can take a good look at your boo-boos. No telling what little Miss Nightingale did to it."

"You're a big liar, Peally," Collette said hotly. "I didn't break anything, and you know it. You broke your own picture frame just to make me look bad!"

Collette stopped — she was breathing so hard

she thought her heart was going to burst right through her chest.

Bending down, Collette picked up her diary from the dirt. She rubbed her fingertips across the sticky cover, staring down at the smudged cat.

It seemed like a very long time ago since it had been brand new.

"I'll wait in the canoe, Roger."

"Oh, look at little Collette going bye-bye with her little kitty-cat diary," sang out Peally in a high, sing song voice. "Now don't go away mad, Collette . . . just go away."

Collette kept walking, concentrating on making her steps even and quick. She kept her shoulders squared, not wanting Peally and Tommy to see the least bit of weakness in her. She squinted her eyes, blinking hard against the tears she would not allow to fall. She wasn't going to let anyone as mean as Tommy or Peally ever see her cry.

Collette stepped into the canoe, throwing the diary onto the seat next to her. The diary's spine split open as it slid along the seat.

Collette picked it up, her eyes glued to the last entry.

...maybe now he will ask me to the banquit!

Collette's eyelids started to tingle. She blinked hard, shivering as another wave of sadness splashed over her.

How could she ever have wanted to sit next to Tommy anyway? He wasn't so —

What?

Collette picked up her diary and studied it closely. Her finger traveled down to the last sentence, leaving a dirty smudge under each word. She flipped through some pages, reading the changed entries. This wasn't what she'd written at all! Peally had rewritten a lot!

Collette hopped out of the canoe and ran back up the hill.

"Peally, how do you spell *banquet*?"

Peally gave Collette a sour face before she shrugged to show it wasn't worth answering. "Come on, Tommy. Let's get going."

"How do you spell *banquet*?" Collette asked again.

This time Tommy looked up, frowning at Collette.

"What is this? Twenty questions? What's the capital of North Dakota? Name seven prime numbers. . . ."

"You are such a creep, Collette," Peally muttered. "Speaking of banquet, Tommy, I'll go early tomorrow night so I can save us a table in the back. Then no one will bump into your leg."

"Spell it," shouted Collette. She didn't care how silly she sounded. Peally thought she was so great, so powerful at the camp.

Roger and Tommy looked from Collette to Peally and back again.

Collette held her diary out to Tommy, pushing it into his hand.

"I did not . . . write this . . . not all of this . . . see this page." Her voice came out in spurts like a car running out of gas.

Tommy opened the diary, glancing in confusion at the last page. Nothing registered on his face.

"Yeah, so what?" He went back to the page,

reading it again. After a second, his eyes met Collette's. He turned to the first page, then back to the last.

Slowly Tommy looked up, then over to Peally.

"Spell *banquet*, Peally."

Peally put both hands on her hips and gave Tommy a big grin. "Aw, come on, Tommy. . . ."

But when he didn't smile back, she gave an angry sigh and crossed her arms.

"This is so juvenile! I can't believe you are playing their stupid game, Tommy. . . . Oh, okay, banquet. B-A-N-Q-U-I-T . . . Satisfied?"

"You spelled it wrong in the diary, too," said Collette quietly.

"Ya-hoo!" shouted Roger. He grabbed the orange flag from Tommy and waved it around and around in the air like a lasso. "One point for the good guys."

Collette stood, both hands at her sides as Roger ran around her in circles, hooting and hollering. She looked up, watching Tommy toss the diary down by Peally.

"Here — it's more yours than Collette's now." His face was filled with anger. "I can't believe you conned me like this, Peally. You lied to me. I bet you broke my fishing rod, just to frame Collette!"

"Hey . . ." Peally wailed, her face collapsing. "You aren't going to believe her, are you? Collette deliberately changed the spelling because she knew — "

"Stop it!" Tommy shouted. "Listen to yourself! Your lies are getting so stupid it's . . . embarrassing. You knew how much that rod meant to me. You were just jealous because I wouldn't let you use it."

Peally's mouth fell open, and a small whine slid out.

Tommy turned, waving her away. "Go on, get out of here."

Behind him, Collette could see Peally, wiping the tears away with the backs of both hands. Part of Collette instinctively wanted to say, "Don't cry. . . ."

But the other part, so bruised by all Peally's scheming, didn't have the strength to speak up at all.

"Get out, Peally. Leave," repeated Tommy.

"*Banquet* with an *E*, *banquet* with an *E*!" Roger

sang out as he lifted both arms in victory. "I love it, I love it. Two points for the good guys!"

Collette rubbed her forehead. Her whole face seemed to ache. Two points for the good guys sounded like a victory. But whoever said victory was sweet must have won a different battle.

"Exit stage left, sweetheart," directed Roger. He stood beside Peally, his left arm extended toward the hill.

Peally shoved past him, slapping down his arm. "Beat it, creep," she snapped, as she turned to leave. "You three deserve each other."

Collette shook her head, not wanting to hear any more from Peally or Tommy. She turned to the canoe, anxious to get back. Anxious to be anywhere but on this island.

"Collette, wait," called Tommy. "Hey, I am really sorry about . . . about everything. I can't believe how wrong I was."

Tommy stopped, looking at Collette for some sort of a signal to go on. Collette knew he wanted her to help him with his apology, to smile or nod and let him know she was already forgiving him.

But she didn't. Let Tommy see how it felt.

Tommy sighed. "I never even asked for your side of it." He reached out as if to touch her, but he let his hand drop to his side instead. "I'm a real jerk."

"Pretty stupid, man," Roger agreed. "I told you this Murphy chick was heads above all that cloak-and-dagger stuff."

Collette almost smiled. Roger could be a pain in the neck sometimes. But he was a pretty good friend all of the time.

Not like Tommy.

Collette looked up at Tommy. It was sad knowing she would never feel exactly the same way about him. Part of the specialness had just flickered away.

"I guess I don't rate any more pages in your diary, do I, Collette?" Tommy gave a weak smile, but his eyes looked really sad, as though he knew he were telling the truth.

Before Collette could even answer, Roger grabbed at her elbow, pumping it.

"Hey guys, let's get a move on. Tommy has to

get to the nurse so I can have my shirt back. I was planning to wear that to the banquet Friday. I'll have to wash it out in the lake."

Roger picked up the orange scarf, dusting it off before he tied it around his forehead.

"I am warning you guys that I am turning into a party animal tomorrow night," Roger sang out as he jitterbugged his way down to the canoe. "Let's go volleyball!"

"Hey, Rog!" called Tommy. "Get back here and lend a hand to the needy."

Collette picked up the green backpack and stood closer to Tommy. "Go ahead, you can lean on me."

Tommy stretched out his arm, then took it away. He shook his head.

"Thanks, Collette, I'm really too heavy for you."

Reaching out, Collette picked up his arm and stretched it across her shoulders. She took a step closer and put her arm around his waist.

"Go on. I'm a lot stronger than I look."

Tommy nodded, his lopsided grin spreading up one cheek.

"I guess I found that out."

Roger scrambled back up the hill, saluting them both.

"Aye-aye, sir. Co-captain Roger Friday reporting for duty. The boat has been made ready for our departure."

Roger ran to the other side of Tommy and wrapped his arm around his waist.

"All together, now . . . walk, walk, walk . . ." directed Roger.

Nobody talked for the first five or six steps, concentrating on the hill and Tommy's leg.

"So . . ." Tommy cleared his throat. "So . . . I was wondering if you still wanted to go to the banquet with me Friday?"

"Sure," Roger shot back. "I mean, you were a jerk today, old buddy, but all is forgiven. Wash my shirt out and . . . let's party."

Tommy swung around to look at Roger. "No . . . I was talking to. . . ."

Roger's face reddened for a second before he shrugged and grinned. "Hey, I knew that!"

Collette knew both boys were looking at her, so she bent her head down and studied the ground.

"Correct me if I'm wrong, Mr. Hansley, but I

believe Collette and I just saved your life, or almost. Anyway, we did knock some sense back into your head about Peally."

"I owe you," Tommy replied with a grin. "You two are a great team."

Collette reached across Tommy and pulled Roger's scarf down over one eye. "The three of us may have lost Games Day, but we are still a great team."

Tommy smiled. "Yeah, a lot of help I was."

Collette shrugged. "You *did* slow us down some. But we are still a team."

"Still a team," repeated Roger. "Boy, I know I've heard that somewhere before."

Collette laughed as they all stopped beside the canoe.

"I think the three of us should all go to the banquet together. It will be a lot of fun."

Tommy looked down at Collette. He still seemed a little worried.

"Even me?"

Roger scratched his head. "I don't know. You were a real jerk. . . ."

"Roger!" Collette laughed. Then she stopped

and nodded her head. "I think we're a team. We saw it through."

"Hey, this is going to be great," Tommy said. He swung his bad leg up and hopped into the canoe. "The banquet is always the best part of camp. The food is pretty good, the sound system is great, and the counselors are in a great mood because they get paid."

"Ya-hoo!" Roger cried. He broke away and gave a furious little dance on the tips of his toes. He whipped off his scarf and waved it up to the sky. "To the banquet!"

Collette started to laugh. "To the banquet," she agreed. She laughed harder at the wonderful sound of it. "To the banquet with an *E*!"